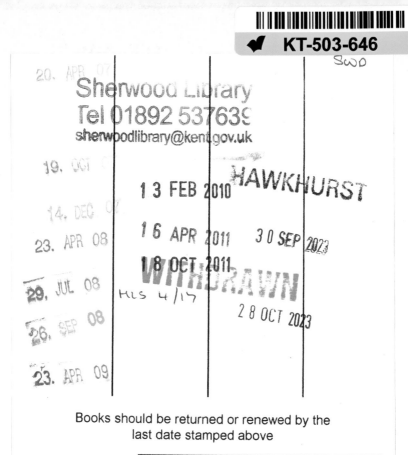

SUSPICIOUS HEART

Chantelle Wilde is a research interviewer for a film company, driving to Villefleurs in the South of France to interview the film star Heloise Remondin. But after she is hit by another car, the handsome driver, Phillipe Blanchard, insists on helping her to repair the damage. When she arrives at Madame Remondin's, she's surprised to discover that he is her grandson. Although she'd vowed never to love again, she hadn't reckoned with the arrogant Phillipe Blanchard.

JOYCE JOHNSON

SUSPICIOUS HEART

Complete and Unabridged

LINFORD
Leicester

First published in Great Britain in 1993

First Linford Edition
published 2006

British Library CIP Data

Johnson, Joyce, *1931 –*
    Suspicious heart.—Large print ed.—
Linford romance library
1. Love stories
2. Large type books
I. Title
823.9′14 [F]

ISBN 1–84617–493–7

Published by
F. A. Thorpe (Publishing)
Anstey, Leicestershire

Set by Words & Graphics Ltd.
Anstey, Leicestershire
Printed and bound in Great Britain by
T. J. International Ltd., Padstow, Cornwall

This book is printed on acid-free paper

1

Chantelle tucked her thick, blonde hair behind her ear and dialled the Antibes number. 'Please, be there, Betsy,' she breathed, her smokey-blue eyes bright with anticipation, visualising the sunlit pool, the villa, Pierre's oceangoing yacht in the marina.

'Hello?' The familiar, dreamy voice of her best friend drifted down the line.

'Hi, Betsy. It's Chantelle.'

'Chantelle! Where are you phoning from? Are you still in Africa? I got your card.'

'No, I'm home. I came back a couple of days early. The rest of the unit's still there.'

'How was it?'

'A bit harrowing, but the film's good. It'll be in the autumn schedules. You mustn't miss it.'

'Do I ever? What's the next one?'

'You'll never guess, Betsy.' Chantelle grinned. 'Background research on Heloise Remondin.'

'The film star — Forties' and Fifties' films? But she hasn't made a film for years.' Betsy sounded puzzled. 'I wouldn't have thought she was Newsworld's scene.'

'Not normally, but listen,' Chantelle interrupted, words tumbling out excitedly. 'Apparently one of our investors — I don't know who — it has to be kept secret for some reason — is a great fan. He wants us to make a birthday tribute. She's seventy.' She paused for dramatic effect. 'She lives in Provence, not a million miles away from Antibes, so I thought . . . '

Betsy's shriek of delight made Chantelle hold the phone away from her ear.

'You're coming to visit! Fantastic! It's time you saw your god-daughter again.'

Chantelle laughed delightedly at her friend's enthusiasm. 'I'm dying to see her. How is she?'

Betsy groaned in mock despair.

'She's a real handful. She was asking when Tella was coming again. When will you be here?'

'Probably Friday. I'm driving south tomorrow. I'll spend a couple of days with Madam Remondin, depending how forthcoming she is and then I've a weeks' holiday — so Antibes, here I come!'

'I can't wait. I'll get Pierre to fix a cruise — an extended boat party.'

'Betsy.' Chantelle's voice was stern. 'Remember our pact — no more matchmaking. No more dates, blind or otherwise, or I don't come.'

'Me, matchmake?' Betsy's tone was one of outraged innocence. 'I wouldn't dare — not after last time!'

Chantelle couldn't help giggling.

'It was a bit of a disaster, wasn't it? Poor chap — what was his name again? Marc Dupont? He was as uncomfortable as I was. We just didn't hit it off. It's always like that, though, when you're conscious that you've been thrown together in the hope that you'll

3

be ideal soul mates. Honestly, Betsy, it doesn't work. Please, believe me, I'm very happy and perfectly contented being single. I don't want to get married — I don't need a mate!'

'Huh!' Betsy sounded sceptical.

Her own marriage to the handsome, rich hotelier and restauranteur, Pierre Deschamps, and her life in Paris and Antibes with their young daughter made her so deliriously happy that she couldn't wait to prod her friend into the same state. But after the Marc Dupont affair, Chantelle had put her foot down. No more attempts to pair her off — or no more Antibes visits.

Betsy sighed.

'You don't know what you're missing, but OK, just the family and maybe one or two friends.'

'Just make sure that they're all happily married.'

'Got it.' Betsy didn't sound convinced, but she knew her friend only too well. Once her mind was made up . . .

'Chantelle, drive carefully.' She sounded anxious. 'You're a bit of a demon in that car of yours. Francine needs a godmother who's going to live a long time.'

'Safe as houses. She'll be arranging my hundredth birthday party. Give her a big hug from me until I arrive there to see her.'

'I will. Take care.'

Chantelle put down the phone and pulled out her suitcases, only recently put away after the African trip. Being a research interviewer for Newsworld, an independent film company specialising in social conscience documentaries, she was often exhausted, like now, having just completed a gruelling month with a unit in remote African villages, working on a documentary about their endemically high infant mortality rate.

Chantelle's work was her life. She'd made that a conscious decision years ago and never regretted it, though the subjects she had to research were often emotionally draining, forcing her to develop a protective thick skin against the tragedies of poverty and oppression which Newsworld exposed and documented.

Offering a silent prayer of thanks to Newsworld's rich film fan, whoever he was, for giving her such a break, she packed her bags happily, with hot sunshine and Antibes in mind. What a welcome change from deprivation!

Betsy was right. It was a most unusual assignment. Chantelle knew that Tim, her boss, would never have agreed to tie up precious resources to film a birthday tribute to an ageing star, without considerable pressure.

At her final briefing, his grumpy impatience was barely concealed.

'It's all a bit odd. The 'fan' insists on anonymity but he's very influential, apparently, especially in Europe. I believe he's the one behind the season of Remondin films coming up on television on Friday nights. I suppose that may boost interest a bit. One angle you can explore is why she suddenly dropped out of the limelight and glitzy glamour in the late Fifties to become a recluse in the South of France.

'It was a seven-day wonder — a real mystery. Just a very elusive whiff of scandal and then nothing! Just when she was at her peak. There may be a good story there, if you can get her to talk about her past — but the main slant will be to examine what sort of a life she lives now, having been such a phenomenal star. Regrets. Hopes. You know the sort of thing. She's probably more than a touch eccentric,' he added unkindly.

'Tut, tut, that's a bit jaundiced. Perhaps you should have a break. Why don't you go instead?' Chantelle's blue eyes were mischievous. She knew very well it wouldn't appeal to him at any price.

'Ugh,' he snorted. 'No thanks. I'm not as nutty about France and all things French as you are. Hey,' he said, brightening considerably, 'maybe you'll catch a nice rich Frenchman — one with a villa in Antibes, like your friend. Then we'd all have somewhere to spend our holidays. It's high time you were settled.'

Chantelle bristled and quickly rose to leave the room.

Even in the unchauvinistic and enlightened offices of Newsworld, it seemed a conditioned reflex to assume that she needed a man in her life, especially at the ripe old age of twenty-eight . . .

As soon as Chantelle approached Dover, she felt the familiar elation and sense of adventure flowing through her.

Driving down the hill to the docks, she practically sang out loud. The magic never failed! There was the usual frisson of excitement as she eased her car into the yawning belly of the ferry, before stepping out on to the deck to watch the English coast slip away.

The May weather couldn't have been more splendid. It was clear and sunny, perfect for a holiday. From Calais, she drove on down the autoroute, pushing her powerfully fast car well south before considering a stop.

Heloise Remondin lived in a tiny hamlet, unmarked on the main map. The nearest village, a mere dot, was Villefleurs. Chantelle's appointment was for the following morning, so Villefleurs seemed an ideal place for an overnight stop.

She took her exit off the autoroute and was soon deep in the heart of rural France. It was enchanting, the blue light of a spring day fading a little towards a softer grey. She passed through small villages where no soul stirred, and shuttered houses belied any sign of life. The names were unfamiliar and her route became circular. At last, she had to admit she was lost.

On the opposite side of the road she saw a small bar with a couple of tables and chairs outside. Swinging across, she parked, went inside and was soon put right on directions. Villefleurs was only twenty kilometres down the road, after a tricky left turn.

She climbed stiffly back into her car.

Relieved to be near the end of her journey, she put the car into gear, glanced over her shoulder to check the road, and slid out. As she turned to face forward, she gasped with horror. Hurtling straight towards her was a long, sporty, red streak. Slamming on her brakes, she braced herself, cursing her moment of inattention, driving out on to the left hand side of the road. She closed her eyes. The red car had come around the corner at speed, but she was on the wrong side of the road. Even if no-one was hurt, she foresaw endless recriminations.

It seemed an age before the crunch came. Surprisingly, it was only a gentle bump, followed by the sound of breaking glass. The red car must have a skilful driver. She waited for the torrent of French fury, mentally rehearsing, 'Sorry, my fault, I'll pay for the damage . . . '

The red car, its long bonnet almost locked on to hers, was, to her amazement, empty, the driver's door flung open. Her heart lurched sickeningly as she realised the driver had been thrown out and was lying on the ground, head under the wheel. This was far worse than she'd imagined. She opened her own door, the blood draining from her face at what she might find.

The driver, a male, was now crouching by her left bumper, and at her approach, he stood up. He was tall, well-built, and his thick, black hair and dark glasses gave him a menacing look. A strong, brown hand removed the glasses as he spoke, in perfect English.

'Not much damage to your car. A broken bulb. I can fix that. Are you all right?'

She blinked in astonishment. The merest trace of French accent gave his voice a sexy undertone. A pair of dark, silver-grey eyes looked at her with concern, not the anger she had been braced for. She swallowed nervously — he was very good-looking. Chantelle's eyes were drawn to his face in fascination, but she dragged her gaze away as she tried to find her voice.

'Are you all right?' he repeated, taking a step towards her.

'Ye . . . es. Thanks. I'm sorry, it was all my fault. I shouldn't have . . . '

The grey eyes gleamed a soft pewter. 'Don't you know better than that? Never admit blame in a car accident.'

'I know that — but it was my fault. It was a perfectly stupid thing to do. I wasn't concentrating, though that's no excuse,' she added hurriedly.

'You're not used to driving in France, perhaps? On the wrong side of the road?' His eyes teased her, a slight smile playing round his mouth.

He's patronising me, Chantelle thought, treating me like a schoolgirl. She flushed, unaware of how prettily the apricot blush sat on her satiny cheeks.

'I've driven in Europe a lot. It's just — well, I'm tired maybe — and I was lost.'

'Lost?' His mouth curved upwards. 'Where are you heading?'

'Villefleurs, but it's all right. I asked the way at the bar. It's not far. I'll go now.' She was still clutching the door handle. 'If you're sure there's absolutely no damage to your car.'

'Not a bit. It's a tough vehicle. But you can't go until I've fixed your headlight. You'll need a new glass, but I'll change the bulb — it'll be dusk before you reach Villefleurs. You've got spares?'

He came nearer. Chantelle was glad the car door was still between them. 'No. Please, it's only twenty kilometres. I'll find a garage. I've delayed you long enough.'

'I know where Villefleurs is. You're not going on without your lights in working order — or without a cup of coffee. You've had a shock. It wouldn't be safe for you to go on. Get your spare bulb pack. You do have it, I hope? It's the law here.'

'I know.' She was nettled at his assumption that she was unaware of the most elementary things. 'I've got it, but really, there's no need, it's only a short distance . . . ' She stopped. The penetrating grey stare was steely, the strong face stern.

'The bulbs!' It was an order. 'And back your car off the road. Over there.' He indicated a parking space by the side of the café.

Mutinously, she did as she was told. Who did he think he was, ordering her about as though she was some sort of incompetent? She wondered about him. He looked out of place on the quiet country road. A businessman of some sort probably making for the autoroute. She parked her car and got out.

Perfectly capable of changing her own light bulb, she thought it wiser not to antagonise the owner of the red sports car. He was standing in the doorway of the bar, his frame more than filling it, talking to the patron. She held out a pack of bulbs and both men looked at her, the patron of the café with amused interest, but the tall man had a different expression in his

14

mercurial eyes. They held an awareness of her as an attractive woman, an appreciation of her slim waist, generously curving figure, and shining hair. She'd seen the look before in men's eyes. It acted as a warning, and usually she knew just how to freeze off that interested male glint. But this man's assessing stare mesmerised her, made her breath catch at the back of her throat.

'Here.' She handed him the spare bulb pack snatching back her hand to avoid his touch. His smile was polite, ordinary, making her think she'd imagined that other look. Hallucinating from hunger, maybe. It was an age since she'd eaten anything.

Disconcertingly, he appeared to have read her thoughts. 'Coffee and croissants. We'll have them outside. It's still warm, and I've been inside all day.' He strode off towards her car.

He's obviously used to having his own way, Chantelle thought rebelliously. What if I want to go inside? She didn't — the evening air was deliciously soft and balmy, the sun still warm, only just beginning its final slide towards the horizon. But it would have been nice to have been consulted!

The coffee was hot and strong, the croissants warm and fluffy. She bit into one with a satisfied sigh and closed her eyes in bliss. Watching her with an amused silver glint in his eyes, the man opposite picked up his coffee and sat back in his chair.

'How long is it since you ate?'

'This morning,' she replied through a mouthful of crumbs. 'On the Dover ferry.'

'You left Dover this morning?'

She nodded.

His eyes narrowed as he looked at her speculatively. 'You're lucky you weren't stopped for speeding. You must have hurtled down here.'

He sounded disapproving and Chantelle bristled. 'I didn't speed. The autoroute's fast. It was fairly empty and I didn't stop. It's not that far,' she added defensively.

Dark eyebrows rose. 'Far enough for . . .'

Chantelle paused, the last piece of croissant halfway to her mouth, eyes challenging him. *If he adds 'for a woman driver,' I'll hit him!* She knew she was a fast driver, and had taken her fair share of teasing about it but she loved driving, and knew she was skilful and safe — until now!

Their eyes locked, hers suspiciously wary; his — again that unfathomable look with its hint of something deep and scarey. Then it vanished, mockery in its place.

' . . . for one day's drive,' he finished innocently, but Chantelle guessed that wasn't what he'd meant to say. 'Are you always so defensive? Your car is a good machine. I'm sure you usually handle it perfectly.'

If only he hadn't added the *usually!* Chantelle gritted her teeth, but his smile was attractively disarming, and she felt ashamed of her resentment. She was being unnecessarily bitter, erecting barriers for no reason. Here she was, in France, being entertained by a good-looking Frenchman who'd been charmingly casual about an accident which was all her fault. It was an adventure, the sort she usually relished, all part of the fun of travelling abroad. But there was something about this particular man which made her uneasy.

'I'm sorry.' She tried to smile. 'But even today, you'd be surprised how many men look askance at women who enjoy fast cars.'

'Very chauvinistic. Not Frenchmen, surely?'

'All kinds! You're French? Your English is perfect, but there's a trace of . . .'

'Of accent? Yes. I'm English — and French. Or maybe French and English. It all depends where I am. But you are most definitely English with that complexion and hair. A beautiful English rose.'

Chantelle blushed.

'Even better,' he murmured. 'I'm

18

Phillipe Blanchard. And you?' He reached over and took her hand in a formal handshake.

She replied automatically. 'Chantelle Wilde,' but her hand sprang to a fiery life as he held her slender fingers, registering a warmth which lasted long after he let it go.

'Chantelle? A French connection?'

'Not really. Only that my parents loved France. It was my mother's fantasy to be French and my name was the nearest she could get. They spent a lot of time here on holiday.'

'Spent? Not now?'

'Both dead,' she said shortly.

Even after fifteen years, the memory stabbed. Their sudden deaths within twelve months of each other had scarred her in her early teens. The subsequent traumas of those years she firmly clamped down. The past was buried. Her present persona bore no resemblance to that painfully shy and insecure young girl whose world had been shattered, just when she was at her most vulnerable.

She saw sympathy in Phillipe's expression.

'It was a long time ago,' she said briskly, and changed the subject. 'I'm surprised there's no damage to your car. You've been very good about it,' she conceded. 'Most men would have jumped at the opportunity to harangue a woman driver.'

The shrug of his shoulders was a pure Gallic gesture, which rippled the muscles beneath the fine silk shirt.

'You have a poor opinion of men. As for the car, there's the merest scratch. Nothing to worry about. A broken car can be mended or disposed of. People are more important.' His eyes held hers intently, a knowing perception in them. 'I think your pride is a little dented. You do not like to make mistakes, perhaps? But it's such a small matter. What matters is that your beauty is unharmed, your face unmarked. Think how it would have been if the windscreen had broken — flying glass . . . '

He was leaning towards her, speaking caressingly, his eyes reflecting a silver made hot by the last rays of the setting sun. 'Now that would have been a tragedy. Your lovely English face.' He traced the line of her cheek with his finger, a feathery touch which sent a shiver through her. She couldn't move away, couldn't seem to tear her eyes from his.

Her voice was breathless as she took refuge in practicality. 'I was wearing a seat belt. And windscreens today are shatterproof.'

Phillipe threw back his head and laughed, the strong column of his bronzed throat drawing her eyes. 'Chantelle! You have no imagination, no romance in you. How English. Seat belts and windscreens.' He tilted back towards her, reaching again for her hand. She tried to draw it away, but his other hand encircled her wrist, clamping it firmly in his grasp. She was aware of the stillness of the evening, the deepening dusk merging the shapes of fields, road and hedges, into one. The bar behind was silent, another dark background shape. She should break away.

'Fate has brought us together, Chantelle. You are not the sort of woman who loses concentration, who makes a stupid error. And I haven't used this road for months. Consider the coincidence.' As he spoke, he released her hand.

Her body was relaxed — lethargic, her mind flashing warning signals. He was putting on a very plausible Gallic act. It was as transparent as a dragonfly's wing and it was time for a put-down. She stole a sideways look at him. The hard angles of his face were blurred by the twilight, his mouth had softened, and a thick lock of dark hair had fallen over his forehead. Fascinated, she stared into his eyes; the hot sunset glow had gone, and that made her feel decidedly odd. She marvelled at the way he conveyed such erotic sensuality.

This was totally crazy! She conjured

up the reactions of her friends if they could see her, the forthright, down-to-earth cool Chantelle Wilde, sitting in a remote roadside bar, mesmerised by the eyes of a stranger. It was quite dark now, and a light breeze made her shiver.

Instantly he got to his feet.

'You're cold. We must go.'

He was brisk and decisive. She wondered again if she'd imagined the look. His eyes, as far as she could tell, were now merely friendly and concerned. He put his jacket round her shoulders, and its warmth flooded through her.

'I'm sorry,' he said, 'I shouldn't have kept you so long. You haven't had dinner.'

'The coffee ... how much ... ?' Chantelle opened her bag.

Again his hand closed over hers. 'No. You are my guest.'

His voice held a reproving note and she sensed the haughty pride which fitted well with her first vision of him. A man used to having his own way, a

tough man, not to be tangled with
— but one who could be dangerously
charming, lulling the senses into acqui-
escence, to his will.

'I'll take you to dinner and then . . . '

'No — thank you,' Chantelle interrupted hastily. Her instincts told her to
leave, to get back in control. She
certainly didn't want to be in the charge
of the handsome Phillipe Blanchard!

'Why not? You're hungry. I know
where to go for the most wonderful
food you've ever tasted. The first meal
of your holiday should be an occasion.'

'I'm not on holiday, I'm working!
And I'm sure I can find my own dinner.
Thank you again for being so reason-
able about the accident.' She moved
towards her car, fishing for her keys.
'Could you recommend a hotel in
Villefleurs I didn't book ahead. I
imagined I'd be there much earlier.'

'Villefleurs — but you're not going
there now?' He sounded puzzled.

Chantelle laughed. 'Of course I am. I
have to stay the night somewhere. I

have an appointment in the morning.'

'Where would that be?' he asked gently.

'I don't think that matters much. You've been kind and I'm grateful. Now I'm going. If you don't know a hotel, it doesn't matter. I'll find one.'

'But I asked you to have dinner with me.' The voice was commanding now, sure of itself. 'There's no reason for you to refuse.'

She opened the door of her car and moved to the driver's seat. He grasped her arm to prevent her sitting down, pulling her to her feet to face him.

'Chantelle, you can't go. You do not need to stay in a hotel. My house is close by — after dinner we can go there.'

'What?'

Incredulity made her gasp. How dare he think she would agree to spend the night with him? So that was why he'd been so accommodating about the car! He'd taken her for an easy pick-up! A single woman — and a foreigner

— easy meat! It was obvious now. That charm of his had a purpose — he was an opportunist, and she'd very nearly fallen for it. She'd even considered accepting his invitation to dinner. If he'd been a little more persuasive — if he hadn't mentioned staying the night at his house . . .

'What do you think I am? Let me go,' she spat out in fury.

She tried to free herself, fear now mingling with anger. What had she done? She was alone — only the dimmest light shone from the bar windows. No-one had passed by for ages and if she called out, no-one would help. They would have little sympathy for someone who had appeared to invite trouble, sitting alone in the dark with a strange man. How easily he'd fooled her.

Now he loomed over her. Her first impression had been right — he was dangerous. Taking a deep breath, she tried to speak calmly.

'Please — you're hurting me. Let me

go. Let's . . . ' She hesitated. It was hard to keep her voice from quivering. 'Let's be reasonable. I won't struggle, but . . . '

Her arm was dropped as though it was white hot. He stepped back from her and when he spoke, each word was an ice shard of contempt and disbelief.

'You're frightened of me? You thought I was going to harm you?'

Chantelle's gasp of relief was obvious. 'No, but . . . '

'What do you think I am?' The question was tersely grated, and she felt the cold force of his anger. It was as cold as his previous warmth had been hot.

Irritation replaced her fear. 'I don't know you, or anything about you, but I'm not in the habit of accepting invitations to spend the night with perfect strangers.'

'I wasn't asking you to spend the night with me. I was offering hospitality to a visitor to France, someone I took to be mature and sophisticated enough to distinguish between a man of honour and some monster who preys on women. Someone with perception. It seems I was wrong. There's a small hotel on the right hand side as you approach Villefleurs. It's called Le Dauphin. You will be quite safe there.' The last words were pointedly sarcastic.

Chantelle's anger was directed at both of them; at him, for being so pompous and at herself for being so naïve and stupid, lingering in the first place. She should have sent him on his way immediately. Her stupid indecisiveness could only be put down to the continental influence; she'd be on her guard in future.

Foreign adventure was one thing — asking for trouble another. She wanted to lash out at him, return to the attack, but it would be pointless. A man like Phillipe Blanchard would always be sure he had the last word.

Nodding coolly, she merely said, 'Thanks, again for your help and for the coffee.'

His answering nod was the merest inclination of his dark head. He held the car door for her with icy formality whilst she got in. Then he slammed it shut. Before she could wind up the window, he bent down, his face only inches away.

'Try to remember to drive on the right hand side of the road, Miss Wilde.'

Chantelle pasted a smile on her face and wound up the window. She swung the car across the road and headed in the direction of Villefleurs. Glancing in the mirror, she saw the tail lights of his car already dwindling in the distance, travelling in the opposite direction.

Blast the man! Her French trip had started on a rather sour note — thanks to Phillipe Blanchard.

2

The massive, ornate iron gates of Domaine Remondin were thrown open between the crested arch which spanned the entrance to the property. As Chantelle turned to drive through it, she had to give way to a limousine coming out, whose black, smoked-glass windows gave no clue to its occupants. It looked pretty impressive, she thought curiously, as it swept by without any acknowledgement of her presence from the uniformed driver.

The gravelled drive was wide and long, the beautifully-proportioned chateau at the end of it breathtaking but the black-suited figure standing like a frozen statue on the entrance steps didn't look at all welcoming. Indeed she pre-empted any admiration Chantelle was about to express, by coming down the steps quickly as if to stop her, but

Chantelle was already out of her car, hand outstretched. She spoke in French.

'Good-morning. Chantelle Wilde, from Newsworld. I have an appointment with Madame Remondin.'The woman's unsmiling face tightened even further.

'I'm afraid you can't see her this morning. She has already had a visitor today.'

'She's not ill, is she?'

'No — yes, that is — Madam is not strong, and she's a little upset.' The woman pursed her lips. 'I am Madame Plombier, her secretary. I don't believe she will want to see you today. Perhaps I can make another appointment?'

'I'm sorry — I'd really like to see her, if only for a short while. I've come especially from London.' Chantelle could see her precious days booked for Antibes slipping by, whilst she waited Madame Plombier's pleasure, exploring Villefleurs, which she'd already done before breakfast!

'It's out of the question. You may

telephone later in the day — this evening.' She moved forward as if to ease Chantelle back into her car, but at that moment a rich, melodious voice called from inside the house.

'Marie, what are you doing out there? Monsieur Beaugendre must have gone by now.' Madame Plombier turned quickly.

'Please go — at once,' she commanded in a piercing whisper.

Chantelle stood her ground. She certainly wasn't leaving at this point. The name teased at her memory — she'd heard it somewhere before, and that voice was familiar. Its rich, breathy quality was unmistakable. It had captivated the world in countless old films, so it was no surprise to see, at the top of the steps, framed in the doorway, one of the most beautiful old ladies Chantelle had ever seen. It was Heloise Remondin — no doubt of that.

Her last film appearance had been about forty years ago. Chantelle had seen her in one of her most popular rôles only last week, and had marvelled at the glamour and charisma of Heloise Remondin. That star quality was still with her, and she certainly knew how to make an entrance! Framed in the doorway, tall, regal and silver haired, she looked down on the two women with a frown.

'Well?' she turned to the dark-haired one. 'I presume this is Miss Wilde, from London? Why are you keeping her there on the steps, Marie? We have an appointment.'

'But surely, Madame Heloise . . . after . . . '

Madame Remondin cut in autocratically.

'Do stop fussing. I'm perfectly all right. Good gracious, I can cope with more than one visitor in a morning. I'm not yet ready for the old people's home, nor am I a fragile piece of porcelain.' Marie Plombier looked agonised but stubborn.

'But you were upset, and the doctor said it's bad for you . . . '

'That is enough.' It had to be a brave woman who would argue with that tone, and Marie had shot her bolt. She threw a dark look of dislike at Chantelle, and went stiffly up the steps. 'The small drawing-room, Marie, and could you bring coffee please — for three, of course.' Now her voice was warm and gentle, mollifying. Chantelle could feel Marie's resistance melting, her poker-back relaxing fractionally. Heloise Remondin was a consumate actress. It was second nature, even after all these years!

An hour later, Chantelle felt the interview was going fairly well, although Heloise Remondin was still acting, playing now the gracious interviewee, but there was something missing. Her grey eyes were clouded, her answers distracted, and deep lines of strain ran from nose to mouth. Her heart and her complete attention were elsewhere. Chantelle was mindful of Marie Plombier's last words before she'd reluctantly left them alone. 'Please don't be too long. Madame must rest before her lunch.'

'I can rest after lunch. Now you've finished your coffee, I'm sure you have lots to do.' Heloise had effectively dismissed her secretary.

Chantelle switched off her tape recorder. Madame Remondin hadn't replied to her last question, and was gazing unseeingly towards the shuttered windows.

'Perhaps that's enough for now, Madame. I don't want to tire you.' The fine eyes snapped back into sharp focus.

'I'm not tired, quite the contrary. I will tell you when I'm tired, Miss Wilde. And I'm not an invalid.'

'No — no — I'm sorry, I didn't mean . . . ' Chantelle was flustered and the star relented.

'I'm sure you didn't. Please disregard what Marie said. She is far too protective. An old habit from the past, and one which I don't believe I'll ever be able to break. I'm enjoying our talk, and, if I may say so, it's you who look tired. A bad night perhaps? Maybe your hotel is not comfortable?'

'It's fine,' Chantelle hastened to reassure her. 'It's just . . . ' She tailed off.

It was impossible for her to say that it was just a blasted man on the road! The memory of their encounter had stopped her falling into her usual dreamless sleep.

Somehow he'd revived unwanted memories, nightmares she thought she had under firmer control. The first nightmare had been her parents' death, followed by the bleak unhappiness of living as an unwanted lodger with her aunt and uncle. That was entangled with a later one — of Alan and college. Alan, who'd brought her back to life, unleashing the feelings of her lonely, numbed heart.

It wasn't his fault he wasn't mature enough to cope with the opening of the floodgates. It had all been too sudden. The dam had burst and she had been too demanding. Her body shrank at the memory. He'd backed off, shocked by the responsibility of responding to her ardent love. His last words came back . . . 'I can't take it Chantelle. You're destroying me. I feel . . . annihilated.'

'Miss Wilde?'

Chantelle blinked, unaware that her hand had moved to cover her heart, as if to ease the remembered pain. It was years since she'd felt it, and she knew what had triggered off the memory — her response to that highly-charged Frenchman on the road to Villefleurs. Her experiences in the past had taught her to be wary of life and people.

Her aim, which she believed she'd achieved, was to be completely self-contained. Only then could she be happy and in control. Phillipe Blanchard had to be merely an unwelcome hiccough in the smooth flow of her life.

'Miss Wilde? What is it?'

Alarm sharpened Madame Remondin's voice, and Chantelle wrenched her thoughts back to the present. 'I'm sorry. I was . . . '

'Somewhere else, evidently not very

pleasant. As I said, I think it is you who needs a break.'

Chantelle pulled herself together, reminding herself she had a job to do.

'But we haven't touched on one of the most intriguing subjects — why you stopped so suddenly in mid-career to retire, to disappear to . . . '

'Bury myself in rural France.' Heloise Remondin completed the sentence with a smile which lit up her face, and Chantelle felt a jolt of recognition. Those eyes! They were so familiar thanks to all those old films she'd steeped herself in to prepare herself for the interview!

'I can't imagine that the public today would be the least bit interested in my motives so long ago. They have so much else to think about nowadays. Ah, here's one of my reasons.'

She broke off with relief, or so it seemed. Whenever Chantelle ventured a question about her past personal life, the great actress had adroitly and purposely evaded it.

'Joelle, come in. Meet Miss Wilde.' Heloise Remondin held out her hand, looking fondly at the tall, slim girl with a cloud of dark hair who had slipped quietly into the room. 'My ward — Joelle Vivier.'

Chantelle was puzzled. Her research had turned up very little about the film star's private life, and nothing about a ward. In any case, Joelle couldn't be more than eighteen — Madame Remondin had quit the screen over thirty years ago.

'Family reasons, you see,' Heloise continued, 'and no, I'm not going to talk about them. Your film, I understand, is to be about my work in the past, and my life now in France, not my personal past. That's one of the conditions we agreed.' She pursued her lips and looked at Chantelle, her expression shuttered. 'Now I want to talk to Joelle. Come to dinner tonight — you'll be company for her. Informal — six thirty prompt.'

The interview was clearly at an end.

Chantelle was being dismissed with an unexpected invitation. Two in two days! There was no question of refusing this one, however.

'Thank you. I'd like to.'

'We'll talk some more tomorrow, too. I've photos, scrap-books and the like which may be useful to you. And I expect you'll want to see more of the chateau and its grounds. Joelle, see Miss Wilde out and then come back here to me.'

Joelle did as she was told, ushering Chantelle before her, shying away from any attempts at conversation. Opening the front door just wide enough to allow an exit, she whispered a soft, 'Good-bye,' and shut it firmly.

'Is it all right if I . . . ' Chantelle completed the request to the empty air. ' . . . look around the gardens now?' She shrugged. Dinner with Joelle and possibly the stern Madame Plombier didn't promise a wild evening.

Still, it was a perfect day and her spirits rose as she looked around. The

Remondin estate would make a glorious setting for the film. Her professional eye swept over the soft-rosy, stone terraces and thick walls, trailing with wisteria and bougainvillea. The house stood tall and elegant, four storeyed, capped at east and west with the round fairy-tale turrets of a picture book chateau. At one side, a long conservatory ran its length and behind that acres of vineyards rose gently to a deep-blue sky.

She walked towards the conservatory. There was no-one about. She peeped in; lemon trees and indoor vines, thick with early clusters of grapes, stretched from end to end. Half hidden by greenery, a man, in the blue dungarees of a farm worker, stood on a pair of steps, pruning a vine.

'I'm sorry,' Chantelle apologised, 'I didn't mean to . . . ' Her throat constricted, cutting off the rest of the sentence as he turned round. 'You!' she managed to gasp. 'What are you doing here?'

'I might ask you the same question!'

Phillipe Blanchard, eyes hooded, looked down at her. She noticed his wellshaped hands, long, supple fingered. Under the dungarees, he wore a sleeveless black T-shirt, his muscular forearms gleaming like polished mahogany. He held a pruning knife loosely at his side.

'I'm here on business.' She was defensive. 'I came to the chateau to see Madame Remondin.'

'You've seen her?'

'Yes — just now.'

'And she gave you permission to lurk about the house?'

Chantelle reacted hotly. 'I was not lurking. I thought . . . '

'You thought you had a right to invade Madame's privacy — inspect the house and grounds?'

'No, of course not.'

'Then you have permission?'

'No — yes — look, this is ridiculous. There's no need for this interrogation. If you must know, I asked if I could see the grounds, but the young girl, Joelle, didn't hear me.' She resented having to explain herself to Phillipe Blanchard, whoever he was! She wished he'd come down from the steps. He was tall enough to give her a crick in the neck, looking up at him, without the added benefit of another few feet! But he seemed perfectly happy to remain there.

He folded his arms. 'So, you've met Madamoiselle Vivier and, no doubt, Madame Plombier, too. A busy morning! Perhaps you'd like to view the vineyards, too?' A faint smile curved his mouth, but never reached the eyes.

It was unbearably hot. The house had been cool, with tiled floors, long windows shuttered. She had not taken off her linen jacket, but now she wished she had.

'There's no need, thanks,' she spoke shortly. 'I can see them myself — another time.'

'You're coming back? What for?

'I think that's my business. Do you work here?'

'Sometimes.'

To her relief, he stepped off the ladder, only to move it nearer to where she stood. His brief look at her was dark, saturnine, and she glimpsed the menacing touch she'd detected at their first meeting. He jumped back on to the steps to deal with the sprouting vine.

She was glued to the spot, her legs unable to function, to get away, out of the conservatory and away from the hypnotic Phillipe Blanchard. He was too close to her. She saw the dark hair of his bare forearms. He looked different from the suave urbanite on the road. Here, in the exotic, rural setting of the old French house and its grounds, he took on a more earthy, primitive charisma, that called out to her bemused senses just as strongly as it had done on the previous evening in the bewitching dusk. The luxuriant foliage seemed to reach out to engulf her, the hot musky scent catching her in the chest, the strong planes of the man's face fascinating her. A warmth, unconnected with the semi-tropical heat, began to suffuse through her. In a moment, she was sure, she would faint, the atmosphere was so oppressively charged.

'I'll go then,' she managed to say.

'As you wish, Miss Wilde.' Even his voice had changed subtly. Yesterday, his accent had been slight, sophisticated, Parisian. Now, it had broadened, was slower. His dark, previously immaculately-groomed hair was casually untidy, with thick locks springing in all directions.

'I'm sorry I disturbed you.'

She seemed to have taken firm root amongst the plants, and her heart plunged as he stepped down and moved towards her.

'You didn't,' he murmured, a steely gleam in his eyes. The pruning knife sheered upwards as he looked at her, and sliced off a wayward green shoot.

Chantelle turned and fled back to the car.

* * *

45

At the small hotel in Villefleurs, Chantelle listened to the tapes of her morning's interview and tried to work out a format for the next day's questions. To her intense irritation, it was Phillipe Blanchard's voice she kept hearing in her head — husky, with a deep sensuality which made her toes curl. The more she tried to immerse herself in Heloise Remondin, the more the image of Phillipe swam before her. What terrible luck that she had to run into him at the Remondin's!

Finally, she abandoned her work, took a long, foam-filled bath, washed her hair, manicured her nails, but the distractions brought no relief. Finally, she flung herself down on the creaky, old-fashioned bed, and tried to face facts.

So — you met a very attractive, undeniably good-looking Frenchman — nationality irrelevant! You've met lots of good-looking men before, so why go weak at the knees about this one? Chemistry? Since Alan, she'd been in strict control of her emotions. So what had gone wrong now? It surely couldn't happen again — could it? She forced herself to face the very worst years, with her aunt and uncle. The lack of affection, the restrictions, the sheer dullness of it all.

When she finally got to college, the freedom, the relief, were so great that when she'd met Alan, the tensions and frustrations of years burst, overwhelming him in the end. She could see now what a burden she'd placed on his young shoulders. Wanting assurances of love for ever and ever, she'd lost him, because she'd expected too much from him.

He finally fled to America to escape the responsibility of her despair. Chantelle had wept and mourned in an abandonment of agony and grief for the loss of love, had refused to eat and had failed to turn up for lectures or the end-of-year exams. Failure by default meant the end of college and no degree! She didn't care. She shamelessly wrote begging Alan to come back to her.

In the end, she'd been lucky. A friend made her go to a counsellor, who persuaded Chantelle back to health and the college authorities to give her another chance. But it had been touch and go. She'd had to take a year out, painfully rebuilding her life, and she never forgot that experience.

Finally, she'd immersed herself in work, got an excellent degree, and joined Newsworld. After that, recovery was rapid, but, inevitably, scars were deep, and barriers had to be erected; a cool aloofness hid a lack of confidence in her own judgements where relationships were concerned. She went out with men, but kept it light, and froze off any serious intent. It was all nicely under control — until that wretched Frenchman had appeared to upset her equilibrium.

Just thinking it through was good therapy. She felt clearer in her head. It was unlikely she'd meet Phillipe Blanchard again. Even if he did work on the estate, it was surely large enough for her to avoid him. At least now she knew she was still vulnerable, which was a valuable lesson. Stronger, higher barriers were needed, that was obvious.

She dressed carefully for dinner with Madame Remondin. A variety of outfits in her luggage had been chosen for the glamorous nightlife of Antibes. Her favourite, a dark-blue, silk dress would barely skim her knee and was obviously not suitable for the Domaine Remondin! A simple, black, sleeveless top and filmy skirt of floral chiffon reached more decorously down to mid calf, her slender waist clipped in by a wide belt. To complete the suitably demure image, she gathered her hair off her face into a high knot.

'That'll have to do,' she said to her reflection, rather wishing the evening safely over and out of the way. 'Don't forget, it's work, my girl.' With a final nod in the mirror, and she picked up her car keys.

Hard work it was, too, she reflected an hour later, as she, Heloise Remondin and Joelle sat in an impressively-furnished drawing-room, its shutters thrown back to let the late-afternoon sun gild the ornate plaster ceiling mouldings. At least the gloomy Madame Plombier wasn't to be a dinner guest. She'd joined them for a thimbleful of sherry, said very little, frowned a lot, then, to Chantelle's great relief, had disappeared.

Heloise had complimented Chantelle on her appearance, then lapsed into silence, seemingly miles away, a growing sadness in her expression ageing her handsome face. Joelle refused to be drawn into anything other than monosyllabic replies. Chantelle sighed, gave up trying to keep a conversational ball rolling, and allowed the silence to settle. It was nearly eight o'clock — and no sign of dinner.

She had a healthy appetite and hadn't

eaten since breakfast. Her stomach rumbled and Madame Remondin was prodded back to the rôle of hostess. She announced, 'We won't wait — we'll go in to dinner.'

Eagerly, Chantelle sprang to her feet — action at last!

'Lovely,' she cried, over brightly.

'I'm sorry.' Heloise looked guilty. 'You must be hungry. We were waiting . . . '

Relief and pleasure chased the sadness and pre-occupation from her face as the double doors were thrown open.

'At last! Where on earth have you been?'

Chantelle's heart flipped violently, and all desire for food left her. She groaned inwardly and despairingly, as Phillipe Blanchard's tall, muscular frame filled the doorway. Dark trousers and an immaculate white dinner jacket made the most of broad shoulders, slim waist and long, lean legs. His wide smile was open and friendly. She frowned at him; he continued to smile at them all, coming over to Heloise, kissing her gently and taking her hand in his with a protective gesture.

'I'm sorry, dear, I was delayed. I know you hate me being late. You shouldn't have waited for dinner.'

Joelle went across to him and he kissed her cheek, putting his other arm round her shoulders, his fingers teasing the floating clouds of curls. The three of them, welded as a group, faced Chantelle across the room.

That was it! The eyes. It wasn't only on the screen. Phillipe Blanchard and Heloise Remondin had the same volatile, mercurial, silver-grey eyes. They had to be related.

'Chantelle — my grandson, Phillipe. Phillipe — Miss Wilde has come to talk to me about the film.'

'I know. We've met — last night, on the road to Villefleurs.'

'Why didn't you tell me this morning at breakfast? I told you she was coming. I mentioned her name.'

Phillipe shrugged. 'It didn't seem of

any consequence.' His steel eyes met and held Chantelle's in a level look. 'I offered hospitality to Miss Wilde last night. It was late and her car needed a small attention. She chose to mistake the intention. I put the incident out of my mind.'

Chantelle felt a surge of anger. He was still on his high horse. And why hadn't he told her who he was that morning? Was he playing some sort of cat-and-mouse game — punishment for not leaping gratefully into his arms last night!

A sardonic smile quirked his lips. 'You see, Chantelle,' he said, his voice lingering on her name, 'it was no sinful bachelor pad I was enticing you to — but the family home I share with my grandmother and Joelle.'

'How was I to know that?' Chantelle asked the question sweetly, but there was a razor edge to her tone.

'Feminine intuition, maybe, should be able to recognise honourable intentions. Or perhaps,' he added smoothly, 'your profession has handicapped you.'

'Why do you say that?'

'You're in the film business, aren't you? Perhaps it's hard to find integrity there.'

Chantelle bit her lip. She had a job to do, and she was a guest in his, or his grandmother's, house. Taking a deep breath, she said quietly, 'I don't think that's fair. I'm not exactly in the film business. Newsworld makes serious documentaries.'

'It's very flattering, of course, but I wouldn't call a birthday tribute to my grandmother a serious issue. Is it really worth disturbing her peace?'

'Isn't that up to Madame Remondin?' Chantelle's eyes flashed sapphire fire.

Joelle shrank against Phillipe and Chantelle noticed his hand tighten on her shoulder. The tension crackled across the room. Heloise looked curiously at them both, then tapped the arm of her chair, cutting commandingly through the static.

'That's enough. I know you dislike the whole project, Phillipe. Heaven knows, you've tried hard to persuade me not to allow it — but, this once, I'll have my way.'

Both pairs of grey eyes locked, hard as flints, and Chantelle saw the anger in Phillipe's before his lids came down. His mouth tightened, but Heloise remained steady, and when he opened his eyes again, the expression was hidden, tension betrayed only in the tautness of the cloth across the shoulders of his dinner jacket.

'And there's no need to be rude to Miss Wilde,' Heloise rebuked mildly. 'She's our guest.'

He looked directly at his guest, coolly and leisurely assessing. 'So she is,' he said pleasantly, leaving no inch of her unsurveyed. 'If I've been rude, I apologise. Let's go in to dinner. Joelle, will you escort Grandmother?'

Chantelle repressed a desire to giggle. All four of them were capable of walking into a dining-room. Escorts, formal processing in to dinner she thought, had gone out with Heloise Remondin's old films!

Phillipe frowned at her as he stood aside to allow Joelle and Heloise to pass, and she turned the giggle into a discreet cough. After all, if they wanted to play bygone days, it was all grist to her professional mill.

The next second, logical thought deserted her. Phillipe had put his hand on her bare shoulder, drawing his fingers slowly to her elbow, before taking her arm in a more formal gesture. His touch, his closeness, sent a sweet tide coursing through her veins — a feeling so long unfamiliar, that the shock of its strength made her gasp. She felt the imperceptible halt in Phillipe's stride, a tightening of his grip, then he was leading her into the dining-room.

Throughout the dinner, as she watched him play the charming host, she couldn't get rid of the feeling that they were all playing a scene from one of Heloise's films. The four of them sat at one end of a table designed for two dozen guests. The cutlery, glass and china were exquisite, and the meal was served discreetly by a dark manservant and a maid. It was like being in another world!

But as she drank the delicious wine and managed to force down some food into her churning stomach, Chantelle relaxed a little. Phillipe encouraged Heloise to reminisce about her film star past in such an amusing way that Chantelle longed for her tape recorder. She was annoyed that he suspected her intention.

'By the way, this is not for public consumption, Chantelle. It's off the record. You know I shall vet the film before its release?'

The hauteur was back with a vengeance, but it was the only sour note of the evening. Even Joelle put several sentences together and confided to Chantelle that she may be thinking of taking a college course.

Heloise reacted sharply. 'There's no

necessity. I need you here. Besides . . . '

A flashing look of understanding passed between Joelle and Phillipe, and he interrupted quickly. 'Grandmère, Chantelle will not be interested in that old family argument. Let's have coffee — in the drawing-room.'

This time he had his way, and Heloise retired defeated, but not before she had made a regal exit.

'I'll go to bed, if you don't mind. It's been a tiring day.' She held out a hand to Chantelle. 'Thank you for coming. We'll continue our talk in the morning. You must stay here tonight — and for the rest of the time that you need. Phillipe will fetch your things from the hotel.'

Panic-stricken, Chantelle tried to protest. 'No — I couldn't! It's too much trouble. I . . . ' She was quelled with a look which brooked no argument — a rôle Chantelle had seen her play so many times on film!

Phillipe looked on in sardonic amusement as his grandmother swept from the room. He stretched, put his hands behind his head, tilting back his chair.

'Grandmère's orders,' he said. 'Coming to the hotel with us, Joelle?'

'No — thanks. I'm tired, too.' She turned shyly to Chantelle. 'I'm glad you're staying.' Her smile embraced them both as she bent to kiss Phillipe.

Chantelle was horrified at the feeling that shot through her as Phillipe kissed her back on the mouth. 'If I must stay, I can fetch my own things,' she said desperately.

'Nonsense,' he cut in curtly. 'We'll fetch them together. Good-night, Joelle. I'll see you tomorrow, before I leave.' He touched her hair again, and Chantelle, with a sick feeling in the pit of her stomach, wondered exactly what there was between them.

3

He drove to Villefleurs at top speed in silence. Chantelle settled her bill and transferred her luggage. On the way back, Phillipe was more relaxed and the beautiful car purred along the narrow roads. The night air was soft and scented through the half-open windows and Chantelle settled back, but the sports car was all body, with not much passenger room. The man beside her seemed awfully close. She avoided his eyes, but as his hand, changing gear, brushed her thigh, she felt a shiver run through her.

'Just the two of us, Chantelle. Where shall we go?'

She shot upright. 'Back to the house,' she said, shortly.

'It's a little early to be tucked up in bed.' His soft laugh in the darkness was teasing. 'I know what we'll do . . . hold tight.' His foot pushed hard on the accelerator and the car shot forward.

Chantelle thanked her stars for seat belts as the car roared its way through the lanes.

'What on earth — where are you going? This isn't the road back to the chateau!'

There was a glint of white teeth in the darkness. 'No, it's not. You have to travel a little way for what I have in mind.'

'But it's half past ten!'

'So? You're not Cinderella — and I shan't turn into a rat at midnight. Well, maybe I might.' His voice was provocative, a note in it which made her spine tingle.

'Turn round at once.' She tried the stern voice which had always worked wonders with her recalcitrant young god-daughter.

Phillipe just laughed again. 'Come on, let your hair down. You behaved as though you were treading hot bricks all the way through dinner. Now you're with me, you can relax!'

That's the last thing I can do, she thought as she caught sight of the speedometer. At least they were on a wider road, although the signs flashed past so quickly, she had no idea where they were.

'Phillipe Blanchard, stop at once.'

'Can't stop here — not allowed. We're on the autoroute.'

'This is abduction. You can't do it.'

'I am, though. This is exactly what you thought I had in mind yesterday. So I'm making it come true. You are totally in my power — for better or for worse.'

His voice had an authority that unnerved her, but what unnerved her more was that maybe she was beginning to enjoy this mad rush to wherever. She mustn't let go.

'You're an idiot,' she said, in a feeble attempt to maintain control.

'Probably,' he said laconically. 'Here we are — Cinderella's Ball!'

They had turned off the autoroute and Chantelle saw that they were driving up a long, tree-lined avenue to what seemed to be a floodlit chateau on a hill top.

'Where . . . ?'

'Chateau des Étoiles. Equivalent of a roadhouse in England — only a bit more gracious. Come on — I can't wait much longer.'

'What for?'

Chantelle got out of the car and he took her hand, slamming the door and pulling her along the gravel path, up wide, stone steps. He pushed the heavy door which opened on modern, well-oiled hinges. She gasped. English road-house! This was more like Castle Fairy Tale.

In the marble-tiled hall, a dark-suited man immediately stepped forward, arms outstretched, to greet them, kissing Phillipe extravagantly on both cheeks.

'Phillipe — how wonderful to see you. You don't have a reservation? No, I would have noticed. Not that it matters. There will always be room at Les

Étoiles for you and your . . . ' He acknowledged Chantelle's presence with a bow. ' . . . lovely English companion,' he finished, with a welcoming smile.

'How does he know I'm English?' Chantelle hissed.

'Long practice,' Phillipe said out of the corner of his mouth. 'Claude, we've had dinner, so just a table — and a bottle of Dom Perignon.'

Claude's eyebrows disappeared into his hairline. 'Evidently a very special companion. This way please.'

They followed him into a large room, as elegant as the entrance, where dining tables spilled out on to an outdoor, lamplit terrace. Dance music was playing and several couples swayed together, caught up in the magic of the balmy evening and the subtle tempo of the music.

'Here, Monsieur Phillipe.' 'Here' was a table, screened by trees in tubs, giving an intimate privacy. The blossom was heady, and Chantelle felt her blood rising in response to the warm enchantment of the atmosphere. Claude beamed. 'My lovers' corner,' he announced proudly. 'The champagne follows instantly. Enjoy the evening.' He glided off.

'What's left of it — and we are not lovers. Whatever made him think that?' Chantelle's blue eyes flashed as she prepared to sit down.

'Oh, no, you don't.' Phillipe pulled her into his arms, and held her closely to his chest.

The shock was electric. Her whole body zinged out in amazed, frightened, delight. She gasped like a swimmer at the first icy contact with a deep, cold river. But she didn't feel ice — her body felt fire as it went its own way and curved softly to his. For a second, neither of them moved. She tilted her head back, her heavy hair rippling down her back.

His grey eyes smouldered. 'This is what I couldn't wait for,' he murmured, his lips close to her ear, 'to dance with you!'

She tried to pull away, but he held

her more closely. Their steps were in perfect harmony, the music moving them together, but the tempo of their bodies was the strongest beat, impossible to ignore. Chantelle felt her eyelids droop, her will dissolving. All her carefully-erected defences were in danger of exploding, blowing away her protective shell.

The music stopped, and the dancers moved off the floor, but all Chantelle heard was the musical sighing of the distant pines. She opened her eyes; the black night was sequin-studded silk. Phillipe's mouth was so close to hers she could watch its curve and, unaware, her own lips parted involuntarily.

He drew a ragged breath. 'Champagne, I think.' He let her go, but immediately encircled her waist to lead her back to the table in its secluded corner. Phillipe lifted the distinctive bottle from its ice bucket, forestalling a hovering waiter.

'No, I'll serve it myself. A special wine, a unique occasion,' he said.

'Very extravagant.' Chantelle stilled her breathing as he handed her a glass.

'To us, Chantelle — to our first meeting. Tonight!'

'Last night,' she corrected.

'That was not our first real meeting. That was a misunderstanding.' The small frown lines above his nose deepened.

A proud man, who doesn't like to be contradicted, a small voice warned, seeing again the cold hauteur of last night's farewell. She plumped for an argumentative flippancy.

'It was the first meeting — and do stop the Gallic charmer rôle. It doesn't wash with me.' She seemed to have run out of breath and took a gulp of champagne. 'Woweee . . . ' She couldn't help it. 'That's wonderful — what a flavour! It's lovely.'

'So are you.' Phillipe leaned towards her and took her face in his hands. 'And this champagne is to be sipped and savoured, not gulped like that. As you, my beautiful English rose, are to be savoured.' Very gently, his mouth touched hers and held it for a fleeting second. Then he sat back and looked at her gravely.

'There is — something there, something between us. You feel it, too.' It was a firm statement, not a question.

'No! Of course there isn't.' She took a long drink to hide her confusion, then stared at him defiantly. 'Champagne — music — dancing. You've laid on quite an act, but I'm not prepared to play a part in it.'

'You don't know what rôle I have in mind for you.' Phillipe's voice was soft, his silver eyes holding liquid promise, only for her. Chantelle tried to hoist the conversation back to a more prosaic level — anything to stop him looking at her like that!

'Why didn't you tell me this morning who you were, instead of letting me believe you were . . . ' She hesitated.

'What, Chantelle?' He was amused. 'What was I this morning? Last night you had no doubts. I was the unprincipled villain! And now?' he asked softly, touching her cheek, drawing his finger downwards to her chin.

She moved his hand away. 'I don't know.' Her dark eyes were truly puzzled, as she looked at the strong planes of his face, his crisply curling hair.

He stood up. 'If you continue to look at me like that, I can only play one rôle. I must dance with you again. Then I'll take you home.'

Chantelle had no choice but to flow with the evening. They danced again, the fusion of their bodies pounding an individual, erotically menacing beat, practically blotting out that of the band. They carried their champagne to the edge of the terrace, looked out across a starlit valley, and were enclosed in an enchanted world.

Chantelle felt as though her body, treacherously, had injected her brain with a sweet potion which left it incapable of rational thought. She knew the man so close to her was dangerous. Life had taught her not to trust: first, her parents, then Alan. She couldn't invest in that kind of emotional commitment ever again.

'It's well past midnight,' Phillipe finally breathed in her ear. 'If Cinderella is to be in her kitchen at dawn . . . '

Like one drugged, Chantelle looked up. His mouth was tantalisingly close. She summoned her powers of self-discipline, hard earned over the years, and pulled away from him.

'Goodness — I'd no idea it was so late. We must go.' Her voice was over-bright, her eyes glittering too feverishly, and she saw he wasn't fooled. He simply gathered her back into his arms. 'Don't fight it. Chantelle. You can't — it's impossible.'

He sounded so sure of himself, so commanding, that her reflexes kicked into violent reaction, and she broke away.

'Fight what? There's nothing to fight. A few hours dancing in this place — the atmosphere — it's been fun. But that's it. Now it's time to go.'

The look he threw her stripped her soul — brooding, intense and savage. The mouth, soft and romantically beguiling only moments ago, was hard and purposeful, the jutting lines of his strong chin and jaw seemingly etched in stone. His eyes, finely-tempered steel, held hers in the powerful dominance of his will, his hands gripping her shoulders, and she knew she would still bear the marks next day.

'Don't,' she said sharply, but the look had vanished before she spoke, and again she was left wondering whether she'd imagined it, called it up from her own primitive subconscious. His smile was warmly innocent, eyes now a dove grey of concern. He's a chameleon, she thought.

It was late, but adrenalin surged through her. Wide awake, intense and watchful in the enforced closeness of the car on their return journey, she tried drastically to distance herself from

Phillipe by brisk questions.

'What do you do for a living?' She could feel him smiling in the darkness and daren't let her eyes slide to his handsome profile.

'I look after the estate.'

'The chateau?'

'And the land. Hectares of vineyards — a winery — a local co-operative. I'll show you tomorrow.'

'N — no — thanks — but . . . ' Panic fluttered in her throat, and his hand touched her knee lightly.

'Don't worry. A proper guided tour — for the film.'

'I thought you didn't approve of the film.'

'I don't, but if Grandmère wishes it . . . ' He shrugged in the darkness. 'I shall make sure it does her justice.'

'Why are you so against it?'

There was a moment's silence before he spoke.

'Heloise Remondin, the film star, vanished years ago. It was a hard decision for her to take, and no-one knows why she took it. She absolutely refuses to discuss the sacrifice of her career to her family. Sometimes I think she regrets it. I thought it might be painful to resurrect old memories and past successes. She's still a great actress — or could have been. I don't want to cause her pain.'

'You love her, don't you?'

'Naturally. She is my grandmother — but she has been more than that to me. My parents were killed in a yachting accident, with my Aunt Fleur, my mother's sister. I was two — I hardly remember them. Grandmère was always there, like a rock, in spite of the tragedy — losing two daughters, so young. Even after that, she could have returned to her career, but instead she bought Domaine Remondin, and devoted herself to bringing us up, myself, my brother and sister. She held us together as a family — we all loved her.'

'Why did she choose France?'

'Why not? She'd had homes in London and America, but her life there was glitzy, unsettled, rushing from place to place. I think she felt we would be better off out of the limelight. She was right, but it was at her personal cost. And, of course, my father was French. Just as Heloise married a Frenchman, so did my mother, her daughter.'

'You're more than half French!'

'Brilliant conclusion!' He was teasing her.

'Where's your family now?'

'Scattered. A sister in the United States, a brother in Australia. Both married. I have six nieces and nephews on my father's side — countless aunts, uncles and cousins. The chateau is quiet now, but for most of my life it's been full of laughter — and love, because of Heloise. We have a reunion every year. She sees to that. It's a bit like a royal command, but we owe her such a lot.'

Chantelle was envious. She'd never experienced that kind of family life. 'And Joelle?' she asked, too casually. 'Where does she fit in?'

There was a pause, and the relaxed tone tightened. 'Joelle is not a member of the family — and I think it's time this interview ended, Miss Wilde.'

'No, please — I want to know.'

'For the film?'

'No — for me. A large family must be fun. I'm envious.'

He gave a short laugh. 'It is fun, but there are drawbacks — responsibilities.'

'Why were you the one to stay on at the chateau?'

Phillipe sounded surprised. 'Someone had to stay, to keep an eye on Heloise and run the business. I'm the youngest. I try not to be away too long. I've an apartment in Paris — a very suitable bachelor pad for seducing maidens in distress!'

He was mocking her again, and she bristled angrily.

'I wish you'd forget about that. My refusal to leap at your invitation seems to have bruised your male ego.'

'I'll forget it, if you'll drop the Miss Interviewer routine. Why don't you try to sleep — we're still half an hour from home.'

Stifling a yawn, Chantelle suddenly realised she was quite sleepy. The ploy had worked — talking about his background and family had defused the highly-charged tension between them. If she could only keep it at bay until she'd finished her work at the Remondins! Her eyelids dropped . . .

Thirty minutes later, the scrunch of tyres on gravel woke her. Musky male scent was in her nostrils. Her head was buried in Phillipe's shoulder, her arm flung across his chest.

'Oh, sorry.' She sat bolt upright, horrified at the way she'd wound herself round him in her sleep.

'Don't be,' he murmured. 'I liked it, although it did rather slow me down. I had to concentrate hard on the road, when all I wanted to do . . . ' He turned her to him, undid his seat belt and leaned across to release hers. ' . . . was this.'

'No . . . ' Chantelle's protest was

stifled as his mouth took hers. She was relaxed, sleepy, off guard. All the sweet promise of the evening was distilled in his kiss.

'Chantelle!' When he finally broke away, his breathing was uneven. 'You are very beautiful.' Then his tone lightened, and the sophisticated poise returned. 'A better place — another time.' He looked at her speculatively. 'English ice indeed! You're as hot and passionate . . . ' His voice died away, and the silver glance was soft. 'Come on, it's time you were asleep.' He touched the blue veined lids of her smoky eyes, then came round her side of the car to open the door.

* * *

Installed in her room, its antiquity as beautiful as its discreet conveniences were modern, Chantelle felt torn apart. One part of her floated dreamily on the cloud where Phillipe's kisses had put her. That self touched her lips where his had lightly rested at the door of her room.

'I daren't come in, Chantelle — you are altogether more than flesh can stand. I'll see you in the morning.'

As he closed the door, she noticed a narrow band of light at the other end of the corridor. Someone in the household was still awake.

Chantelle's other self tried hard to punch holes through the cloud. Will you never learn, she chastised harshly. Life isn't to be trusted! Men, particularly the Phillipe Blanchards of this world, aren't to be trusted. Her severe self cringed with shame at the memory of her quick response to his body.

Grimly, she dragged her mind back to the past. She'd responded with the same readiness to Alan, and that desperate need had frightened him to death. Destroyer! Annihilator! She made herself say the words out loud, to the mirror. The passion she saw in the dark eyes frightened her. Phillipe Blanchard was not a man to be destroyed or annihilated. He had a hard, mature confidence and would always be in control. More likely he would destroy and annihilate her.

All the hurt and humiliation of her college years flooded back. She had to be strong and avoid any involvement with Phillipe. It could lead nowhere but to more pain. With a despairing groan, she punched the pillows, shut her eyes tightly, and tried to blank out her mind in sleep.

4

She must have succeeded. The next thing she heard was the shutters being flung back to let the sunshine stream into the room. A young girl put a tray of coffee by her bedside, and wished her good-morning. Room service as well. What a life the Remondins led!

She joined Joelle and Heloise for breakfast.

'Good-morning, Chantelle. I hope that wasn't you I heard coming in so late last night.'

Madame frowned her disapproval, and Chantelle was relieved when Phillipe appeared in the doorway to provide a diversion to prevent her answering. He kissed his grandmother good morning. 'Phillipe, I thought you were going to Lyon early,' she exclaimed.

'No — later. I'm going to show

Chantelle the estate this morning.'

'Joelle or Marie can do that. Chantelle is seeing me this morning.'

A steely glint replaced Phillipe's soft smile. He might love his grandmother dearly, Chantelle thought, but he also loved getting his own way. 'As you wish. I have some phoning to do. I'll go to Lyon after lunch, when I've shown our guest around the estate. No, Grandmère, that's the arrangement.' The grey eyes locked again. The younger won, on this occasion.

Heloise inclined her head, but left the room almost immediately, with straight-backed disapproval. 'Whenever you're ready, Chantelle,' she said as she left. Chantelle gulped down her coffee.

'Sit down — drink your coffee,' Phillipe commanded. 'She'll wait for you.'

Her stomach gave a lurch, which didn't help the coffee one bit, as he put his hand on her bare arm. She concluded that the Remondins were a bossy lot and if she wasn't careful, she'd be turning into an acquiescent dreamer like Joelle, who had drifted out after her guardian, after a sweet smile for Phillipe. She spoke acerbically. 'I do have a job to finish. I'm due in Antibes tomorrow and there's still a lot to cover.'

His mobile mouth curved at the edges. 'At noon then. We'll take a picnic and tomorrow I'll take you to Antibes.'

'You'll what?'

'Come with you to Antibes. I have some business there, and I'm due for a break. What are you researching there — a social documentary on the wealthy and over-privileged Mediterranean jet set?'

Chantelle was still reeling. 'I'm taking a holiday, if you must know, seeing my god-daughter. Staying with a friend who just happens to be part of that 'set' you're sneering at — and how you've the nerve to knock wealth and privile . . . '

'There's no privilege here, and any wealth is damned well worked for,' he flashed angrily at her.

'I don't have to defend my friends to you, but they work hard, too — and you're certainly not taking me to Antibes. I'm driving myself.'

'Your car — my car — it makes no difference.'

'But, I've told you . . . '

'Grandmère will be ready for you now. Mustn't keep her waiting.' With infuriating nonchalance, he sat down, opened the newspaper by his plate, and began to read. 'See you at noon,' he said levelly, without looking at her.

With an explosive gasp of fury, Chantelle left the room. She swore under her breath as she picked up her notebook and tape recorder from her room. He was maddeningly irritating. Antibes indeed! What a nerve. But wouldn't Betsy be delighted if she arrived with a handsome Frenchman in tow!

With an exasperated sigh, she went to find Heloise. The estate tour seemed inevitable and she did need to see it for background material — but she wasn't so sure about a picnic by the river!

Heloise was aloof, preoccupied, and Chantelle found it even harder going than yesterday. There was still something very much in Madame's mind. She moved around restlessly, answered questions in monosyllables. Finally, she said, 'It's no good, I can't concentrate. Go and have Phillipe's tour. I'll talk to you after he's gone.'

Phillipe was waiting for her in the hall. 'It's hot — don't forget a swim suit.'

'I don't think I've time to come . . . ' she attempted.

'Don't be so silly. Hurry up, I've only got a couple of hours.'

'You don't have to . . . '

'Chantelle . . . ' He moved towards her, giving slow emphasis to each word. 'Go and get the bikini you've obviously brought specially to knock out the Antibes glitzies — and stop being difficult!'

He gave her a gentle push towards

the staircase, impatiently raking his fingers through his dark hair. He'd changed into shorts and T-shirt and his muscular, brown legs drew her eyes as she went up the stairs, vowing to be cool, calm and distant for the next two hours.

Of course he made that impossible. He was outside when she came down again. A motorbike stood incongruously outside the old chateau! Phillipe handed her a crash helmet.

'Tuck up your skirt — I forgot to tell you to wear shorts. Hop on and hang on to me.'

She barely had time to perch on the pillion and put her arms loosely around his waist, before he'd started the motor and roared off down the long drive and out on to the road. The momentum nearly flung her off and she had to grab hold of him more tightly. He turned and laughed at her over his shoulder, even, white teeth gleaming in his tanned face, black hair tousled by the wind.

'That's better,' he yelled.

She moved away from his back as though he were red hot. 'You're to show me the estate,' she shouted desperately.

'OK.' He slowed down. 'Vineyards over there, peach plantation by the base of the hill, cherries and an olive grove beyond. You'll see them when we reach the top.' They breasted the hill and he stopped, holding the machine steady, feet astride on the ground.

Chantelle cried out in delight. 'It's beautiful — the colours . . . ' Looking back, she could see the chateau nestling among the trees, the tall turrets half hidden, the sun mellowing its old stones. The vines, in young, tender, green leaf, looked fresh and innocent against the dark, almost black, green of the cypresses, planted in long lines like guardians.

'Those are wind breaks,' Phillipe explained, 'against the Mistral — the wind from the north. It drives men mad — like some women,' he added. 'Hold tight, we're going down to the river.' He revved the engine and they jolted down a bumpy, rutted track through fields of vines before he brought the bike to a juddering halt by a river bank.

Chantelle walked slowly down to the water. A riverside picnic! The last time she'd had a picnic was a snatched sandwich in Trafalgar Square, surrounded by people, mobbed by pigeons. She couldn't imagine a greater contrast. Here, it was quiet and tranquil, the scent of pine and tamarisk in the air, and herself and Phillipe the only people in sight. She slipped off her sandals, and dipped her toes in the cool water.

Philippe came up behind her. 'It's shallow here. There's a deeper pool up the path to the right.' He slung a rucksack over his shoulder and took her hand.

It was a perfect spot. Chantelle stood on a flat rock, overhanging the water. A waterfall cascaded over huge stones before running more quietly downstream to form a natural pool, dappled by sunlight to molten gold.

'It's beautiful. One of the nicest picnic spots I've ever seen.'

'One of the nicest!' His eyebrows drew together in a frown. 'It's the nicest. I come here a lot when I'm working on the vines. Do you want to have a swim before we eat?'

Chantelle looked at the crystal water; brown and white stones at the bottom, fish gliding slowly in the sunlit depths. 'Yes, I do.'

She avoided Phillipe's eyes as she took off her skirt and top, thankful she had put on her bikini before she left. So far, so good, she thought. The atmosphere was light and friendly. A swim, a picnic — finish off her work — escape to Antibes tomorrow! She relaxed. The sun was warm on her flesh, and a light breeze fingered her soothingly.

'Is it deep enough to dive?' She turned, poised on the edge, and looking back, she caught her breath.

Phillipe was behind her, blotting out the sun, a dark outline of power and strength. His eyes were dark, intent on her face. He took her forearms, and she could feel his flesh burning hers. He held her gaze while he spoke softly.

'Yes, it's deep enough — if you have the nerve.'

His words were double edged. Tearing her eyes away, she turned and dived into the water. It was as heady as last night's champagne, and closed over her head, before she broke the surface, gasping at the icy cold on her sun-warmed body. Throwing up diamond drops, she swam out to the centre of the natural pool, aware of Phillipe close to her, treading water. Sunlight filtered through the trees, the ageless rocks towering above them. Slowly, he took her shoulders, propelling her gently through the water.

In the natural elements of air and water, time stopped. Chantelle forgot the world, and enjoyed the sensation of cool freedom. They swam lazily, side by side, up the river, then back to the picnic rock. He finally swam away from her, but she stayed, floating, face to the sun, at one with the hypnotic, lulling lap of the water. She didn't want to return to earth, to reality.

A deep voice insisted. 'Lunch.'

Looking up, she saw she'd floated back to the rock and Phillipe was watching her from the top.

When they'd eaten, he stretched out beside her on the sun-hot rock. He drank mineral water, while she sipped a second glass of wine. 'It's a pity you can't have any,' she murmured, squinting down at him. 'It's delicious.'

'It should be — Remondin's best. The grapes are grown not a mile away, and it was made just down the road.' He took the glass from her, taking in the aroma of the wine, swirled it round, and took a long sip, rolling it round his tongue and teeth, sucking in the air. Then he spat out the wine and took a drink of water. 'Not bad at all. Holding up well!'

'Did you have to spit it out?' Chantelle grimaced her distaste, laying back on the rock, senses lulled by the wine and food, eyes closed.

He propped himself up on his elbow. 'Can't risk even a whiff of alcohol on the Lyon autoroute.'

His voice was calmly conversational as he said, 'You must know how provocative you look stretched out on that rock. Like a sleek, beautiful cat.'

She shot up immediately and pulled a towel over herself. 'Sorry, I didn't mean to . . . it's just this spot, the water . . . '

He laughed, and put his arm round her shoulders. 'I know what you mean. It has a magic of its own, and you mustn't be ashamed of being attractive. There'll be other times.' His grey eyes, soft and eloquent, were telling her things she didn't want to know.

'No.' She spoke quietly. 'I'm going to Antibes tomorrow — on my own. I shan't be back.'

He stood up, pulling her to her feet. 'We'll see. I'll be home this evening. We'll talk then.' Lightly his lips touched hers. 'There isn't time now.'

He took her back to the house at high speed, leaving her jolted and breathless. It seemed hours since they'd left the chateau. At the front door, he took her hands.

'Trust me, Chantelle. It's not easy. There are — complications. But trust me,' he repeated, and kissed her lightly on the lips.

Chantelle was in a turmoil. It would be dishonest to deny she was attracted to Phillipe Blanchard, but could she reverse the conditioning of years and trust him, as he'd asked. It was alarming to her that she even considered the question!

'Damn him!' she muttered, annoyed with herself for carrying his image into Heloise's sitting-room with her.

The old lady was sitting, staring out of the window, and when Chantelle came in, she started nervously.

'I'm sorry . . . I thought . . . Come in, come in — I expected you. I was just . . . a long way away.' She turned her shrewd grey eyes to Chantelle, noting the flushed cheeks and bright eyes. 'I trust you had an interesting tour — and that Phillipe was a good guide?'

'Yes.' Chantelle had difficulty in looking his grandmother in the eyes.

'He didn't come to say goodbye.'

'No. He was — late. He said he'd be back tonight.'

'Tonight! Why?' Heloise frowned. 'It's too much in one day. He should stay overnight. He works too hard. Don't you think he's made a superb job of the estate?' she added abruptly.

'Everything looks fine. The vines are healthy . . . '

'Did you see the winery — the co-operative?'

'No, there wasn't time.'

Heloise looked at her suspiciously. 'You've been away for hours. I thought . . . ' She stopped, giving Chantelle an intently piercing look. She continued slowly. 'The estate was derelict when I bought it. Phillipe has transformed it — his wine co-operative is a great success and he's developed a large export market. He didn't tell you any of this?'

'No.'

'But I thought that was the object of the exercise — to familiarise you with the lifestyle here. A contrast to the career I might have had?'

'I can see how you live here — it's charming. Ben, our chief camera man will be in his element. The colours, the scenery . . . ' Chantelle knew she was babbling, but couldn't help herself. She knew also that the eyes, so like Phillipe's, were not deceived. Desperately trying to regain the initiative she asked, 'Madame Remondin, you haven't told me — why did you agree to this film about you? You seem so private here. Won't it be an intrusion into that privacy?'

Heloise frowned. 'I don't see why it should. No-one will know its exact location. As to why, that shouldn't concern you. If you need a reason, call it an old woman's vanity, or curiosity. To have someone who actually wants to have a film made about my life — it's intriguing.'

'You don't know who?'

'No — even Phillipe has failed to discover the identity of the unknown admirer. And your company, Newsworld, can't — or won't — identify him. So you see, my dear, it's rather like living in one of my old films, for a while — a bit of harmless make-believe. I'm enjoying being the centre of attention again. Just for a while.'

Chantelle was listening intently. So Madame Remondin still loved the limelight! That was obvious. So why did she give it all up so many years ago? She left the question unasked, but uncannily Madame Remondin answered it.

'My family was the most important thing in my life, Chantelle. It still is, but that doesn't mean that sometimes . . . ' She tailed off, and paused, looking intently at the young woman sitting opposite to her, noting the sparkle in her eyes, the half smile on her lips. Alarmed, she realised that here was a girl on the brink of love. She came to a decision.

'Perhaps it's a kind of final fling for

me, too, before I retire as head of the household. The chateau, as you see, is a wonderful place now, perfect for bringing up a family. I shall perhaps move to one of the smaller houses after Phillipe is married.'

'Married!' Chantelle's heart juddered.

'Didn't he tell you about that either? He really is too bad. What's the matter, Chantelle? You've gone quite pale.' She put out a concerned hand. 'Phillipe kept you out in the sun too long. It can be very strong at this time of the year.'

'I'm all right.' Chantelle fought for recovery, and was amazed to hear her voice, normal and even, in polite enquiry. 'Whom is he marrying?'

'Joelle, of course. It's their destiny — they've been sweethearts for years. I'm longing for great-grandchildren. Phillipe's only been waiting for Joelle to grow up. The house to be full of children — young life again — it's my dream for the future here at the chateau.'

Chantelle felt ill. Phillipe and Joelle! Their children! Then a tidal wave of self-loathing engulfed her. She'd almost been prepared to fall for his charms, to consider trusting him, to allow herself to fall into the trap — again! What a fool to be taken in by his game! Flirtation was second nature to him and he was as good at acting as his grandmother.

Heloise, too, was playing a rôle — warning her off! She'd succeeded. She wasn't going to give the Remondins the satisfaction of seeing her hurt. Before he came back to witness her humiliation, she'd be gone. Briskly, she opened her note book.

'I'm sure you'll all be very happy. Now, can we get on? I'd really like to leave for Antibes this evening.

★　★　★

Thank goodness for work, Chantelle thought, as she packed away her material. She'd had to concentrate on getting as much information as she needed in the shortest possible time. Madame Remondin, as though relieved of a burden, had been eloquent and forthcoming, stressing her hopes for the future. She would enjoy this coming third cycle of family life at her leisure, she said, without any pressures from the past, or any regrets about abandoning her successful career.

All good viewing stuff, Chantelle thought ironically, still not quite believing the reasons Heloise gave. It was all a bit too glib.

Relieved that she'd managed to finish in time, well before Phillipe was due back, she thanked her hostess and added, 'Congratulate Joelle for me. The camera crew will be down next month. I hope it won't interfere with the wedding.'

'No. It'll probably be in the autumn. Will you be down again?'

'It's unlikely.'

Madame Remondin's expression of polite regret barely concealed a look of satisfaction. Not quite such a consummate actor as her grandson, Chantelle thought later, as she flung her cases into her car boot.

She then got into the car, put her foot hard down on the accelerator and sped down the drive. How could she have been such a fool? Visions of the picnic by the river returned to haunt her. To think she'd almost believed the promise in his eyes. What sham! She hated him for taking her back to the days of her youthful vulnerability.

Halfway down the drive, she saw Joelle, who turned and waved for her to stop. She braked sharply and wound down the window. It wasn't Joelle's fault that she had almost fallen for her fiancé but Chantelle couldn't bring herself to warn her of his behaviour.

'Are you leaving?' Joelle asked in surprise. 'I thought . . . '

'Joelle, tell me — are you and Phillipe Blanchard to be married?'

The young girl's smile faded, and she chewed her bottom lip. 'Heloise! She told you?'

So it was true! It wasn't just an old

lady's fancy — Madame Remondin's dearest wish. It was reality. Soon those fawn-like brown eyes would be looking in adoration on Phillipe's silver grey ones.

'Chantelle — wait — please!'

Chantelle wound up the window and drove on, just as the imposing black limousine with darkened windows turned into the drive. She drew in to let it pass, and as before, the uniformed chauffeur stared impassively ahead, acknowledging neither her nor her courtesy.

The road which eventually led to the autoroute and the Mediterranean was narrow and winding, the same one, presumably, which she and Phillipe had taken to the Chateau des Étoiles. She squeezed her eyes shut to obliterate the memory. When she opened them again, they widened in horror. This was impossible! The red sports car was approaching round a distant bend. What on earth was he doing back so early?

With a feeling of déjà vu, she looked around wildly. There were no side roads, and the chance of his flashing past was unlikely — one car would have to slow down to pass the other. Chantelle drew in to the side of the road, looking grimly to the right, praying he'd pass. He didn't. She heard the door slam. He was out of his car, opening her door. She tried to pull it to, cursing herself for not locking it as soon as she'd seen him.

'Chantelle! Where are you going?'

She sat rigid, gathering up the strength of all her hurt humiliation. Her voice was cold.

'Go away. There's no need to go on with this particular charade any more.'

He held still, but kept his hold on her door.

'Charade? What do you mean? Please, get out of the car.'

'No. Just get back in your car, and let me pass.'

She saw his mouth tighten. 'What's happened? This morning . . . '

'Was all a mistake. I've finished the job I came to do, and I never want to see you, your grandmother — or Joelle, again.' Her voice shook with anger, and she revved her engine.

'Heloise! What has she said to you?'

'The truth. You're going to marry Joelle. Sweethearts for years, she said. Lots of grandchildren in the chateau.'

'Damn.' Phillipe reached down, turned off her ignition, and took her arm.

'Get out of the car,' he repeated. 'We can't talk like this.' She shook off his hand angrily.

'I've nothing to say to you. I asked Joelle, too. This morning — last night — it was all a ridiculous farce. Oh, I'm not so naïve! You're not married yet — nothing wrong with a flirtation — last fling, a bit on the side! But why did you have to make such a big production of it? Dom Perignon indeed. All quite unnecessary.' She glared at him.

The shivers of ice in his voice matched hers.

'Didn't I ask you to trust me?'

'Why should I? I wish Joelle joy of you. I'm sorry for her, but I expect you'll act out the rôle of faithful husband. You're such a good actor, you'll probably get away with it.'

'So you're running away?'

'No. I'm just carrying on with my planned schedule. That doesn't include you. I hope never to set eyes on you again.'

He stepped away from her car, and now his face was dark with anger, his voice bitter.

'Why not? I'm in London a lot. You seem to have cast me as the unprincipled, about-to-be-married philanderer. I expect you'd play the rôle of mistress very well.' The pulse at his throat beat strongly.

'You deceitful, contemptible . . . ' She struggled to find words that would hurt, dent his conceit. Taking a deep breath, she managed to say quite calmly, 'I don't think my fiancé would be very pleased with that arrangement.

I'm getting married soon, too. So this has to be goodbye.'

He went white, and his full mouth became a thin line, grey eyes filled with contemptuous steel.

'Well, well,' he drawled, 'two of a kind. You're as bad as I am, Chantelle Wilde — seems we've both been playing games the whole time!'

He turned and walked back to his car as Chantelle drove off at speed. Neither looked back.

5

Being with Betsy, Pierre and Francine in Antibes had partially helped to soothe Chantelle's anger. Determined not to spoil her holiday, she pushed Phillipe Blanchard out of her mind. Betsy had unwittingly helped by arranging a hectic schedule of sightseeing and socialising. Today, near the end of her visit, was the first time they'd relaxed by the family pool, soaking up the sun and wonderful warm air.

'Tella, Tella — swim — now.'

Chantelle laughed. 'Again? What are you, a mermaid, or something?' Her god-daughter, Francine, a rosy, dark-haired beauty of a toddler tugged her hand, pulling her towards the turquoise water of the swimming pool.

'It'll soon be time for her nap,' Betsy said. 'We've hardly had a chance to talk together since you arrived. You mustn't let her commandeer you.'

'I don't mind. It's one of the reasons I'm here, to get to know my god-daughter again. Come on then, Francine, one final go.' Allowing herself to be pulled along, she and Francine tumbled head first into the pool.

'She's going to be an Olympic champ!' Chantelle gasped as they finally clambered out of the water. 'She's fantastic!'

'She's always loved the water. She swam before she walked. No, Francine, I'm going to take you for a nap — no,' Betsy added firmly as the small girl's lip quivered, and she threw an appealing glance at Chantelle. 'No more swims now. I want to talk to my friend. Don't go away, Chantelle, I'll be back in a few minutes.'

'Where would I go?' Chantelle laughed as Betsy scooped up her daughter and carried her towards the house.

Left alone, she stretched out on one of the loungers by the poolside. Betsy and Pierre's luxurious villa was perched above the town, looking out over the flawless blue of the Mediterranean. Distant, purple-hazed hills curved round the sides of the bay. It was breathtaking, and she feasted on the view, before closing her eyes and lifting her face to the sun.

'Wake up!' Betsy startled her as she plumped down beside her. 'Sorry I was so long. Francine took an age to settle, but she's asleep now.'

'I didn't mean to doze. It's wonderful here. You're a lucky girl, Betsy, having Pierre and Francine.'

'I know. And that's why I'd like you to have the same. It's the best life!'

Chantelle smiled. 'Only if you have the right person to share it with.'

'But you won't give yourself a chance,' Betsy broke in. 'That's why . . . ' She stopped, and bit her lip. 'I mean . . . '

Chantelle sat up suspiciously. 'Betsy, you haven't invited your idea of another Mr Right, have you?'

'Well — not exactly, but . . . ' She

went on with a rush. 'I couldn't help it, it was Pierre. It's his cousin, Michel. He's a film director and Antibes is the setting for his next film. He always comes with us on the yacht. Honestly, Chantelle, I wouldn't have asked him, after I promised, but I can't send him to a hotel just because you're . . . '

'Betsy! Of course you couldn't. For goodness' sake, it's your house. You invite who you want.'

'You'll like him. I'm afraid he's very eligible, good-looking, and great fun. That's why I thought you'd think I'd engineered it deliberately.' Betsy looked relieved. 'Pierre'll be home soon, then we're going out to dinner with Michel, and tomorrow we're going to cruise round the coast for a day or two.'

'Sounds perfect.' Chantelle reached for the sun oil, and started to apply it to her arms and legs.

'That's a relief. I thought you'd hit the roof and accuse me of match-making again. Here, let me do your back.'

'I've come to the conclusion that it's part of your nature and you can't help it,' Chantelle said, with a fond smile for her friend as she turned to lie on her front. 'But don't worry, I'm totally impervious to the charms of the opposite sex at the moment.' Especially after Domaine Remondin, she thought grimly. Never again would she allow herself to be beguiled so easily. All she wanted was to forget the entire episode.

But she'd reckoned without Betsy, who looked at her speculatively, as she replaced the top of the sun-cream bottle. 'You haven't said a word about the Remondin Chateau. Did something go wrong? You're usually absolutely bubbling with your latest project.'

'There's nothing much to tell.' Since Betsy had come straight out and asked her, Chantelle thought she might as well get it over with quickly. 'The chateau is wonderful, Heloise Remondin's still beautiful — a bit frail, though she'd never admit it. There's something sad about her. I don't know what. She has a lovely life, surrounded by beautiful things — fantastic countryside — France! I'd give my eye teeth to live in a place like that.'

'Perhaps she's lonely. Isn't she a bit of a recluse?'

'That's the impression she likes to give. She insists that we don't give away the exact location of her home in the film documentary.'

'Does she live alone?'

'No. There's a startled fawn of a young ward, a dragon secretary, and lots of visits from her family during the year, with a grand reunion at the end of the summer. And there's a grandson, too.' She hesitated before standing up. 'Now, that's enough of the Remondin family. I'm going for a swim. Must make use of your gorgeous pool. I'll think of it when I'm back in London in my pokey old flat.'

'It's a very nice flat,' Betsy said, as she followed. She was puzzled. There was a cloud in her friend's eyes. She was glad Michel's visit had coincided with Chantelle's. It was one of her dearest wishes to see her friend as happily married as she was herself. Better still if she married a Frenchman!

★ ★ ★

Chantelle wore her blue, silk mini-dress, and let her hair fall loosely around her shoulders. Michel Deschamps, Pierre's cousin, was to meet them in one of Antibes' best restaurants. Built practically on the water, it commanded a wonderful view over the bay's azure depths. They were early and arrived before Michel. Pierre put his arms affectionately round both girls.

'This is wonderful. One man, with the two most beautiful women around. What a pity Michel has to come and spoil it!'

'Just as well,' Betsy said severely, 'with Chantelle looking so attractive. If she wasn't my best friend, I'd be jealous.'

Pierre kissed his wife. 'You know,

darling, you have my heart entirely.'

The eloquent look of love they exchanged smote Chantelle's heart. She'd always revelled in her friend's happiness before. The creeping chilliness round her heart was a new emotion, and she was glad of the distraction when a broadly built man with a shock of blond hair approached them, and embraced first Betsy, then Pierre.

'Michel!' Betsy stepped back from his kiss. 'It's lovely to see you again. This is Chantelle Wilde, my friend from England. Chantelle — Michel.'

Admiration flared in his eyes as he took her hand. 'Betsy has often spoken of you, Chantelle. I'm so pleased to meet you. You work for Newsworld, don't you?'

The evening was balm to Chantelle's bruised spirit. Michel Deschamps was every bit as charming as his cousin, Pierre, and an instant rapport was established between the four of them. Michel was interested in the work she did at Newsworld, and entertained them with tales about his own career.

Betsy leaned back and smiled in satisfaction as the two of them plunged into an animated discussion about the technicalities of film making. She chose to ignore her husband's rueful grin and whispered, 'Betsy, stop it — your chickens may not hatch!'

'There's still the boat trip to come,' she whispered back, with a smug expression.

★   ★   ★

Pierre, taking the wheel, nudged his sleek, white yacht out of the multimillionaire's yachting marina of Antibes. Chantelle and Michel were on deck, Chantelle marvelling at the number of huge luxury boats tied up side by side with scarcely a pin's space between them.

Pierre had decided to hug the coast, and sail the short distance to Monaco, anchoring at Nice for the night. Chantelle didn't mind where they went, the scene and the company being sufficiently different to take her mind off the raw spot still throbbing from her last hours at Domaine Remondin.

Michel was a charming companion, and the day slid by in a sunny, blue haze of swimming and sun bathing. Francine monopolised as much of Chantelle's time as she was allowed, and it wasn't until late in the evening that the four adults were alone together for supper on deck. The light had faded to a rosy glow, the air was balmy. A faint shadow of a moon began to rise as they dropped anchor outside Nice. They ate fresh salmon and drank chilled champagne.

'I could get used to this life,' Chantelle murmured.

'We work hard, too.' Pierre sounded just the least bit defensive. He'd built up a chain of restaurants the hard way and, in their early married years, Betsy had helped him, supervising the catering side herself. She was a trained cook, and had been responsible for their delicious supper.

'I know you do.' Chantelle was contrite.

'And,' Pierre broke in, 'I have a little work this evening, too.'

'Pierre, you promised,' Betsy exclaimed.

'It won't take long, cherie. I'm negotiating with a new wine supplier. The owner of the Remondin vineyard is in Nice, so he's coming aboard . . . '

'Remondin! That's where Chantelle's just been,' Betsy said.

'Is it?' Pierre poured more champagne. 'Did you sample their wine? I thought Betsy said you'd been interviewing some old film star.'

Chantelle's throat was dry and, in spite of the warmth of the night, she shivered. 'Who is it you're meeting?' she managed to gasp.

Pierre glanced at his watch. 'A Phillipe Blanchard — should be here at any moment.' He threw an apologetic look at Betsy. 'Truly, it's only a matter of dropping some wine here — but if Chantelle knows him, maybe he'll stay.'

'No, no! I don't want to see him,' Chantelle gasped. 'Please!'

'What on earth's the matter?' Michel put his arm round her shoulders. 'You've gone quite pale.'

At that moment, one of the crew came across the deck. 'Launch alongside, monsieur. Your visitor has arrived.'

Pierre stood up. 'Bring him down here — and another glass, please. He'll surely stay for a drink.'

Chantelle leaped to her feet, sending her chair flying. 'Francine! I promised her a story. I must go.'

'But she'll be asleep — and you did read her one an hour ago.' Betsy looked bewildered.

'I'll just check on her then.'

Michel bent to put her chair upright, and placed his hands on her shoulders. 'Sit down, Chantelle. Francine's perfectly all right.' He pushed her back gently into her seat. 'What are you worried about?'

Phillipe Blanchard, coming down the stairway from the upper deck, stopped abruptly as he saw Chantelle, her blue eyes wide and feverish, staring up at him. He could also see the tall, blond-haired man bent protectively over her, his hands caressing her bare, tanned shoulders.

6

It was a moment frozen in time, a photographic still of a group picture, the varying emotions of the characters caught and held for ever. Then the tableau came to life, with Philippe's incredulous lash-sharp exclamation.

'Chantelle Wilde — here! And . . . '

But Pierre stepped forward quickly to greet his visitor. He held out his hand. 'Monsieur Blanchard, after all our phone conversations, it's good to meet you at last. Please, sit down. You'll have champagne?'

'Thank you, no.' Phillipe made no attempt to sit down, his eyes still fixed on Chantelle and Michel. 'I'm sorry, I appear to have interrupted a private party. I assumed it was to be a business meeting.'

'Just family — and friends. I thought, as we were both in the area . . . ' Pierre hurried on. 'Can't I persuade you to join us for a drink? This is my wife, Betsy, *Michel Deschamps, my cousin, and I believe you've met Chantelle.*'

The icy hauteur of Phillipe's voice struck a chill which cut deep inside Chantelle. He took the glass Pierre held out to him.

'Oh, yes. Miss Wilde and I have certainly met.' The grey eyes were hardened steel, as he acknowledged Michel with a curt nod. 'But I'm afraid I really cannot stay. I have to return to Chateau Remondin tonight. An urgent family matter.' He placed the champagne, untouched, on the table.

Chantelle watched the long fingers, white and taut round the stem before he let it go. Looking down, she found she was clutching Michel's hand convulsively. Throwing a look of proud flashing anger to meet his hauteur, she said, as calmly as she could, 'I hope your grandmother and your fiancée are well — and that my visit didn't tire Madame Remondin.'

She heard Betsy's tiny gasp before Phillipe's cool reply.

'On the contrary, both are well, and Madame Remondin is in better health than she has been for some time.' The thick brows drew together in a dark scowl, then he turned away, and spoke to Pierre. 'As I have so little time, perhaps we could discuss our business elsewhere. I've left wine samples up on the bridge.'

Chantelle dropped Michel's hand, and got to her feet. 'Betsy, I'm afraid I have a headache. If you don't mind, I'll go to my cabin.'

'I'll get you some aspirin.' Betsy looked with concern at her friend's flushed face. 'I should check Francine anyway, so we'll leave you two men to it.' Her voice lost some of its usual warmth when she spoke to Phillipe. Somehow, the man had upset her friend. There was no mistaking the undercurrent of antagonism that flared between Chantelle and this very attractive Frenchman whose appearance on the yacht seemed to have set off an emotional time bomb.

But Phillipe's anger did not spill over to Betsy. His grey eyes became soft as he smiled at her.

'Good-night, madame. I apologise for disturbing your evening. Perhaps we can meet again in more convenient circumstances. I believe you are responsible for the splendid cuisine at the Deschamps restaurants?'

Betsy, disarmed by the compliment, was more friendly. 'Well, not so much nowadays. Francine, our daughter, takes up most of my time, but I do still keep an interest in the restaurants.'

'You must allow me to take you and your husband out to dinner when I'm next in Antibes, to celebrate the negotiating of our successful wine contract perhaps? I'll telephone you, if I may?'

'That would be very nice. We'll look forward to it.'

Chantelle could bear it no longer — that charm act again! It seemed deliberately staged to isolate her. She could sense Betsy being won over by Phillipe's easy magnetism. With a muttered, 'Excuse me,' she pushed past them, and ran down the stairway to the cabins below.

Chantelle remained below, straining her ears for sounds of Phillipe's departure. It seemed some evil quirk of coincidence kept him appearing in her life! At last, there was a roar of a motor. For *someone who was anxious to return home, Phillipe had stayed with Pierre for what seemed an eternity* to her.

She relaxed a little as the sound of the engine faded into the distance but sleep was an impossibility. She felt restless in the small cabin. She didn't feel like answering questions — but surely the others would be in bed now? Betsy had been a dear, but it was clear that her curiosity couldn't be curbed indefinitely. Maybe it would all look better in the morning. It often did, but meanwhile there was the night to get through.

Quietly she made her way up to the top deck. The boat was silent, its living-quarter lights dim. They were anchored off shore but the bright lights of Nice spread out and sparkled, diamond bright along the coast, twinkling up in the surrounding hills. She crossed to the other side of the yacht; the black, silky emptiness of the night sea suited her mood better.

She leaned on the deck rail, seeking consolation from the softly murmuring waves lapping against the side of the hull. The sea was ageless — timeless — a reminder that all mortal griefs must pass and be forgotten. Time would ease the hurt caused by Phillipe.

Michel's discreet cough preceded his presence at the rail by her side. 'Chantelle. How's your headache? I thought you'd be asleep.'

'No. The air's good up here. It's cured the headache. It's gone.' She gave a shaky smile.

'Along with Monsieur Blanchard. Could the two be connected?'

She sighed. 'Was it so obvious?' Michel was silent, and she stared ahead into the starlit night for a few moments before she added, 'I just couldn't hide my feelings, I suppose.' She stood staring over ther dark waters.

'Which were?' he prompted gently.

'Dislike, of course — hatred almost.'

'Hatred! Was that what it was? I shouldn't have thought you capable of hatred, Chantelle. Strong feeling, passionate emotions perhaps — but hatred — no, surely not?'

'Yes.' Her response was vehement. Phillipe had deceived her, played with her emotions and all the time was engaged to be married to Joelle. She couldn't forgive him. 'I never expected, or wanted, to see him again — ever. To see him on board was a total shock.'

'He must have done something very terrible.' Michel's voice was soothing. 'You were only at the Remondin chateau a couple of days, weren't you?'

'That was enough! Michel, I don't want to talk about it. I was stunned when he appeared tonight. I'd hoped Antibes would wipe it all out.'

'It will — whatever it was — and when you get back to London, to your work, it will be better. I'm a great believer in the present and the future — there's no point regretting the past. It's done with.'

'In my head, I know you're right.'

'It's just that sometimes the heart won't always follow the head.' Michel looked down at her shadowy profile. 'If I can help in any way, Chantelle . . . ' He let the offer hang between them in the soft darkness.

'Thank you, Michel.' She turned towards him. 'There is something I should tell you. I feel terribly embarrassed about it.' She hesitated. Although nothing had been said, she knew from Phillipe's face that he'd leaped to the obvious conclusion. Michel's arms had been on her shoulders — she'd clutched at his hand. 'I'm afraid Phillipe probably thought you and I are . . . well, are engaged.'

'How very flattering — for me,' Michel replied gravely. 'How would he get that impression, from the brief minutes he spent with us?'

'From something I said at the chateau. Please, Michel, I can't explain. It's just that if he and Pierre are to have business dealings, maybe sooner or later, you might hear an odd rumour . . . ' She tailed off miserably.

Phillipe had put her in this awkward position. Chantelle was honest, hating lying and was furious with both Phillipe and herself that she'd been so stupid as to invent a fiancé. But she hadn't been thinking rationally when she learned that Phillipe Blanchard was to marry Joelle.

Michel took her hand, and put it to his lips. 'I think, maybe, I understand. Please make whatever use of me you wish. It would be an honour to play the rôle of your fiancé, Miss Wilde.' He spoke lightly, diffusing any awkwardness, and she was grateful to him.

'I'm sure it won't be necessary to go

that far. It was just here. Once I'm back in London . . . '

He interrupted. 'In London, I hope we'll meet, have dinner, see some films together?'

'No, really, Michel, you don't have to do that.'

'But I'd like to.'

'I can't. It wouldn't be a good idea, honestly.'

'As a friend, Chantelle. No strings, as they say. I have to come to London frequently.' Michel chose his words carefully. 'Just because you've been hurt, you shouldn't cut yourself off from the world. You are far too attractive to do that. There are other things, other experiences, other friendships. Life is for living, not for regretting.'

Chantelle looked up to the crescent moon, casting a silver shimmer on the black ocean. Somehow it put things in perspective. Michel was right. Seeing him in London would do no harm at all, and she certainly wasn't going to spend all the rest of her days moping over that deceitful Frenchman from Provence!

'All right, Michel, I'd like that. As long as you understand the situation.'

'I do,' he said simply.

7

Tim tapped the folder on his desk. 'This is very good, although more suitable for a chat show, or a 'Private Lives' series, than a thought-provoking documentary.'

'It is gossip stuff, but that was the brief. I'm sure you can make some social comment on it. You usually do.'

Chantelle, back in London, had concentrated on putting the Remondin material together as fast as possible. Then she could be rid of it, obliterating all trace of the memory.

'You've done a good job, Chantelle. But I have not heard a word from our mystery backer. Maybe he's changed his mind. How was France anyway? Did you find a madly-attractive Frenchman with a holiday villa in the Med?'

'No, I didn't. France, as ever, was fine.'

Tim eyed her keenly. 'Hardly full of your usual enthusiasm. What's happened to our Francophile? I noticed that you didn't bring back the usual bag of smelly cheeses for the office lunches.'

'I didn't have the time.'

'You had a week's holiday in Antibes! What were you doing down there?'

'Tim, why the interrogation? You're not usually interested in details of my shopping trips.'

'Sorry. It's just that you seem a bit down. It's uncharacteristic behaviour after a visit to France. But if it's personal . . . OK, let's get down to the next assignment.'

'Please!' Chantelle's agreement was heartfelt. She hoped it was somewhere on the other side of the world from Europe. Deepest, darkest Africa, at least. What Tim came up with was quite satisfactory.

Briskly businesslike, he pushed a file towards her. 'Forget Remondin for a bit. We'll work out a format for that when you get back.'

'From?' Chantelle took the folder eagerly.

'The States — West Coast. Mexico and California have a big problem with illegal Mexican immigrants. They've been slipping over the border in droves, and it's quite a headache for both sides. The Mexicans are desperately poor, and they're lured by the American dream — which can often turn out to be a nightmare. There are lots of angles to explore. One of the poorest countries, next to the golden state — that sort of thing. All the background's in that folder, plus your ticket to Los Angeles. A couple of weeks should cover the preliminaries.'

Chantelle was already flicking through the sheets of paper, absorbed by the new project. Tim's next words almost failed to register.

'When you get back, we'll send you off to your beloved France, and the Remondins.'

She opened her mouth to refuse, then closed it. No point in stirring up conflict yet. With a bit of luck, Tim might drop the whole thing. He wasn't keen, and the mystery backer didn't seem to be putting the pressure on. Mentally, she crossed her fingers.

Meanwhile, the States job was a godsend — far enough from Europe, and sufficiently different from her last assignment. 'Thanks, Tim. Sometimes you can be an angel!' She left the office with a lighter heart than she'd had for some days.

Time was her friend, and the two weeks flew by. She worked with Tony Price, Newsworld's top photographer and between them they amassed enough material for the basis of a documentary on the plight of the poverty-stricken Mexicans.

In Mexico, Tony filmed the squalid poverty from which some of its citizens were trying to escape. Out with the border guards, patrolling the freeways, Chantelle spoke to many who were caught and sent back. Whole families attempted the hair-raising border crossing, before being engulfed in the busy multi-carriageway roads. The guards told her that some Mexicans were run over before they reached safety, and Chantelle's soft heart wrenched with pity.

On the return flight, Tony crystalised her own thoughts.

'We're so damned lucky. Even this . . . ' He indicated the plastic airline lunch. 'It would be manna to the starving, and we throw most of it away. We've got jobs, pleasant places to live, plenty to eat . . . ' He shook his head. 'So lucky,' he repeated.

Chantelle agreed, suddenly ashamed of the richness of her own life. The Mexican assignment had set in perspective the few days emotional trauma resulting from her encounters with Phillipe Blanchard. The job had acted as a catalyst and, carefully, she set about rebuilding the barriers around her heart, and got on with her life.

There was plenty to distract her. Newsworld's staff was kept frantically busy. Tim sold films to BBC, ITV and

American networks. Further commissions followed. Their reputation was growing, as was their list of projects. The Remondin file mouldered in the cupboard, and Chantelle began to think it had been shelved. It had a very low priority on Tim's list, and it wouldn't upset him in the least to drop it for more universally important topics.

Chantelle's feelings were ambivalent. She knew it was hopeless, but much as she professed dislike of Phillipe Blanchard, a remote corner of her heart wouldn't allow her to forget that current of feeling that had charged through her at the Chateau d'Étoiles, and at that enchanted picnic spot by the river. In all honestly, part of her had to mourn the setting aside of the Remondin project, with its fairytale chateau setting.

Michel Deschamps provided another distraction. He was in London to set up a financial deal for his latest film, and he and Chantelle went out together on several occasions. He kept his word.

Charming, attentive, an attractive escort, he never attempted to kiss or even touch her. She had been nervous about accepting his invitations out. Her heart, guarded though it was, was still bruised, and didn't need any more challenges! But Michel behaved impeccably.

On his last evening in London, she offered him supper at her flat. She went to a lot of trouble with the menu, and Michel brought champagne and Burgundy. The evening was relaxed and pleasurable, and in the final stages, they took coffee and brandy into Chantelle's elegant living-room.

He looked round appreciatively at the clean lines of the décor and the furniture.

'You obviously have a talent for home-making, Chantelle. And for cooking! That was a truly delicious meal. Almost as good as my cousin-in-law, Betsy.' He laughed but the mention of her friend made Chantelle suddenly nervous. She nearly spilled the coffee she was pouring. 'Betsy doesn't — you haven't said anything . . . ?'

'No, no. Don't worry. Your secret's safe with me. I haven't seen Pierre and Betsy since we were all in Antibes.' He took the cup from her and poured brandy into two crystal balloon glasses. 'Actually, it's quite a pleasant idea, once you're used to it. I've never been a fiancé before. A husband, yes . . . '

Chantelle looked alarmed. 'You're not a fiancé. I told you. What happened to your wife?'

'We parted, years ago. Mutual. I've been very careful ever since. But this week, Chantelle, surely proves that we can be good friends, with no strings. You're an extremely attractive woman, but we don't have to complicate a friendship!' He handed her the brandy glass.

'No, we don't. Thanks, Michel. I've enjoyed this week, too.'

He ran his hand through his thick blond hair, then picked up the TV remote control. 'Do you mind if we see the news? There was talk of an airport strike.'

'No, of course not.' Chantelle was relieved. A danger moment had passed, one she'd probably imagined anyway.

They caught the end of the news, with no report of plane delays, but Michel flicked through the channels before switching off. 'Hey!' He stopped and held the station. 'Isn't that Heloise Remondin, your documentary star? It's 'Princess In Exile,' her last film. Isn't she beautiful? Those eyes! May I watch or ... ' He looked shrewdly at Chantelle. 'Can't you bear it? Perhaps you're still on the boil from whatever happened when you were at her chateau.'

She shrugged. 'I don't mind. I've seen this one before — it's nearly over but we'll watch it through to the end if you like.'

They settled back in the deep sofa. There was something very cosy and companionable about watching an old TV movie with a friend, after a good dinner and wine! Tonight Chantelle felt she could watch Heloise objectively, without the remembered sharp pain of association with her grandson. She congratulated herself as she watched the closing scenes of Heloise's final film.

It was a fairly predictable romantic type of fairy-tale, old-fashioned now, but with a naïve sweetness and sincerity that Chantelle could see was appealingly different from modern-day cynicism. Set in an imaginary late nineteenth-century mid-European country, it had a timeless theme — the hardship of choice. Heloise, looking far younger than her late thirties, played a princess in love with a commoner. Her choice was simple. Exile with her loved one, or exile from love, following the path of duty as future queen. No question in those days!

Chantelle sighed. 'Poor thing,' she murmured, but Michel's eyes were rivetted to the screen.

In the final frames, the princess said goodbye to the great love of her life.

Chantelle recalled the scene and remembered originally assessing it for its technical expertise, rather than for its emotional power. That was before her visit to the Remondin chateau! Now she saw another dimension. Heloise was electrifying! As she embraced her handsome, young lover, her eyes held a great depth of poignant sadness and despair which was truly tragic. Saying farewell to her love, she stared down the lonely chasm of bleak duty ahead.

The film was still in black and white, and its grainy texture enhanced the stark quality of the emotion. Chantelle pressed her fingers to her lips. As the lovers tore apart, the young man backing slowly away from the door, Heloise, in an agonised cry, put out her hands, her whole body taut with the tension of not running to him. Chantelle felt the strong will which rooted the princess to the spot. As the commoner went out of the door, the camera closed in on Heloise's face, her eyes brimming with tears, her face ravaged with sadness. The director held the shot for ten seconds, then faded into the closing scene — the coronation of the princess as queen.

Then the face turned to the unseen, unknown audiences of forty years later. It was stern and regal, but in the eyes, the same deep emotions were expressed — sorrow, despair, and in a final jolting flash, bitter anger — anger that such a choice had been forced upon her.

The music crashed appropriately as the credits rolled. Michel clicked the auto-control and the screen blanked. Chantelle blinked away the tears, and swallowed a lump in her throat.

Michel laughed. 'I'd like to get that reaction to one of my films.'

'I know it's ridiculous, but — that last scene!' Chantelle felt breathless. 'Either she's one of the best actresses in the world, or she's living out on screen what actually happened in her life. The princess had a choice and was furious that she had to make it. It must parallel Heloise's own life!'

'Wasn't her choice even simpler? Career or family?'

'Trust a man! It's never that simple, I imagine. I wonder, in her case. Was it a straight choice? That's what she presented to the public, but I feel there's more to it. I don't think she wanted to give up. She loves the limelight, and the sense of being in charge.' Chantelle remembered the clashes of will between the old lady and her grandson. Heloise had been used to being centre stage. 'I think she was forced to give up, by someone — something.'

Michel drained his brandy glass and stood up. 'You've been seeing too many romantic, old movies. In Paris, I'll show you some of my films — much more realism!'

Chantelle replied slowly, 'I'm not sure I'd like those as much.'

''Course you would. You're a modern girl, with your eyes wide open to reality, not that fairy-tale stuff.' He picked up his jacket. 'I've got to go — early flight tomorrow. Thanks for dinner, and I mean it about Paris. I would like to see you again.' Placing his hands on her shoulders, he stared down into her blue eyes. It was several seconds before he said softly, 'Perhaps you should go back to the Chateau Remondin, to find out about Heloise — and to follow your own heart! It's still in Provence, isn't it?'

'No, it's not possible.'

He kissed her lightly on the forehead. 'Anything's possible today, if you want it badly enough. The question is how badly do you want it?'

As Chantelle closed the door behind him, she realised she dare not answer his question.

With a curious sense of fatalism, she entered Newsworld's offices next morning. A note on her desk called her to Tim's office. Two of the company's latest recruits were with him when she went in.

Her boss threw her a strange look. 'Well, Chantelle, it looks as though we're forced to complete the Remondin film. Orders from on high! I was hoping it would die quietly, but no such luck. I've put Emma and Pete on it, with you as overall continuity. Pete'll be in charge of the filming. By a lucky coincidence, the big annual family reunion at the chateau is next week . . . '

'Not quite our usual line of filming, but good experience for you both, under the wing of an experienced old hand like Chantelle.' He nodded towards Chantelle, who was gripping the arms of her chair tightly.

'Must I go?' She tried to keep her voice neutral. 'I'm — er — quite busy at the moment. And — I wasn't exactly a number one hit with the family.'

Tim raised his eyebrows. 'That's not what I heard. I've talked on the phone to Heloise, and she especially asked for you to be there for the family party. And, I'm a bit hurt that you didn't tell us — apparently you're getting married.'

Chantelle closed her eyes. Her aunt had always warned her that lies always came home to roost, with dire consequences.

Trust sanctimonious Aunt Dora to be right!

'Er — well, perhaps I can have a word, Tim — later.' Desperately clutching at straws, she said, 'What about Helen? She's a real film buff? She'd love to go.' But she could see that Tim had made up his mind.

'No, she's tied up. We're overstretched, so there's no choice. One more chance for you to go to Provence — and in September, too. Lucky you, I'd say. One more thing. The re-run of Heloise's old films has stirred up a bit of old gossip. I've tried to trace it, but the shutters snapped down pretty fast. There's some powerful influence at work there. But it means you may have some company in Provence — gossip hounds, trying to dig up some dirt. Pete, Emma, that's all. I'd like a private word with Chantelle. Enjoy the trip.'

Chantelle's brain raced. Could she refuse point blank to go? She thought she had her emotions well under control, but to see Phillipe — and Joelle — together.

'Tim, I don't think I can go.'

He cut across her protest. 'So, you're a dark horse. Marriage! A Frenchman, Madame said, with a Mediterranean villa?' he continued hopefully.

Chantelle shook her head. There was no alternative. She told Tim as much of the story as would explain the sudden possession of a fiancé. 'So you see why I don't want to go to Remondin. I feel such a fool — and a fraud.' Her dark blue eyes pleaded with Tim to let her off the hook, but he was briskly matter of fact.

'Understandable, but unprofessional to let a misunderstanding interfere with finishing a job you started. Sounds like a huge party down there, so it's unlikely you'll see much of Phillipe Blanchard anyway. Keep up the fiancé fiction if you like. Anyone I know?'

Chantelle was grateful that Madame Remondin hadn't identified her 'fiancé' as the well-known film director, Michel Deschamps.

'Oh, no,' she said casually, 'just

145

someone I met in Antibes. A good friend.'

She left Tim's office knowing that she had to go back to Remondin. Remembering Michel's words, she shivered. 'You should go back, to follow your heart . . . ' What was the point, when she knew what she'd find there?

8

They flew to Marseilles, hired an estate car, and drove up to Villefleurs in broiling late-summer heat. Chantelle was glad to approach the chateau by a different route, hoping to mask the memory of her previous visit under different circumstances. Emma and Pete helped. They were wildly enthusiastic about their first project for Newsworld, and Chantelle, five years their senior, felt like an elderly aunt!

As they drove up the drive, through open gates, she half expected to see the black limousine turning out of the driveway. Instead, a large blue van practically blocked their way. It was one of many vehicles that were buzzing around the chateau, presumably connected with preparations for the grand celebratory party.

'Wow!' Emma's exclamation was

awed. 'A real picture-book chateau. It's like a film set.'

'Wait till you see the characters.' Chantelle laughed, but couldn't stop the nervous flutters of trepidation, as they parked their vehicle in the grounds at the back of the main building. 'We'd better announce our arrival, then we'll see what's going on, melt into the background, and set up for tomorrow for the big event in the evening.'

She had wanted to stay in the hotel down the road, but Heloise Remondin had invited them, through Tim, to stay at the chateau for the annual Summer Ball and Emma had been so thrilled that Chantelle hadn't the heart to refuse.

In contrast to her last visit, the chateau was alive with activity. At least a dozen cars were parked nearby and as they walked to the front door, they saw several more in the front driveway. They could hear the high-pitched shouts of children playing and away over on the main lawn, a huge marquee was being erected.

Chantelle's heart constricted sharply as a mature replica of Phillipe met them on the steps. His charming grey-eyed smile was so much like Phillipe's that she almost turned and fled! He held out a welcoming hand.

'You must be from Newsworld. Let me give you a hand with that equipment. I'm Jacques Remondin, Heloise's son. My mother has told me all about you. She'll see you when she's rested.' His eyes clouded with anxiety. 'She has not been well, I'm afraid. All this . . . ' He gestured comprehensively round the grounds. 'I hope it won't be too much for her.'

'Perhaps we shouldn't be here,' Chantelle started to say, clutching an escape straw without much hope.

'No, no. Forgive me, I shouldn't have mentioned it. Maman insists in any case, and when Maman insists . . . ' Chantelle gave a rueful half-smile. She knew all about that!

Inside the chateau, it was just as busy. As well as numerous family and friends, an army of professional caterers and florists swarmed everywhere. Chantelle began to breathe more easily. At this rate, Newsworld really would be able to blend into the background and perhaps not even be noticed in the midst of all the activity.

Jacques showed them to their rooms and invited them to a buffet lunch in the garden, to meet the rest of the family. Heloise was in her room resting, but had asked to see Chantelle at once. He left her outside Heloise's door.

'Go in, she's expecting you. We'll see you later, in the garden.'

Nervously, Chantelle opened the door. The bedroom was enormous, with a huge four-poster bed, but Heloise was lying on a chaise-longue by the tall windows. She made no attempt to get up when Chantelle approached, but beckoned her forward.

'Chantelle? Over here please, where I can see you properly.'

The room, shuttered against the midday heat, was cool and dim. The prone figure on the sofa was shadowed, but Chantelle was shocked by what she saw. Heloise looked ill, seemed thinner, her skin transparently white, framed by pale hair, giving her a wraith-like appearance. She was still beautiful, but the grey eyes had a strange glitter in them.

Motioning Chantelle to a seat near her, she raised herself up into a sitting position. It obviously cost her an effort and Chantelle went to help her.

'Thank you,' she said quietly. 'I'm glad you could come. I thought perhaps, after last time . . . '

'I had no choice. Newsworld insisted.'

'You didn't want to?' The sharp eyes were shrewd, assessing.

Chantelle was pleased that any resentment she may have felt towards Madame Remondin had vanished. She simply felt pity for the sick, old lady who was wrestling with some unhappiness in her past. She was sure of that now. It was an intuitive feeling she'd had ever since seeing 'Princess in Exile.'

Heloise was somewhere in her own mental exile, and it was taking a terrible toll on her physical health.

'I had to come. she repeated, 'and I'm happy to be here.'

Heloise sank back with a sigh of relief. 'I'm glad. Now that you're to be married, too.' Chantelle's heart wrenched at the 'too.'

'I had to see you, to make sure and to congratulate you. I hope you'll be very happy. I've been so worried. I imagined you were . . . forgive me . . . falling in love with Phillipe. That, of course, would have been impossible. He and Joelle . . . You wouldn't have done at all. Marie wouldn't have allowed it. If we don't obey, the consequences . . . ' She shuddered, her eyelids closed, and her head dropped to one side.

Chantelle leaned forward in alarm. 'Madame — Marie? Who . . . ?'

A severe voice behind her made her jump. 'You've over-tired her. How dare you come in here!' Madame Plombier glared at her as she bent over Heloise.

'I didn't. I was brought here, by Monsieur Jacques,' she said quickly. 'Madame wanted to see me.'

'Umph! Well, she's seen you now. Fortunately, she's asleep.' She picked up one of the bottles of pills by the sofa bed, and clucked disapprovingly. 'She's under mild sedation. If she rests now, she'll be able to attend the family supper.' Banging down the bottle, she said violently, 'I wish they'd all go away, and leave her in peace!'

The wish patently included Chantelle, who left as fast as she could, wondering which of the relations milling around the chateau was Marie, and why the redoubtable Madame Remondin was so frightened of her.

Chantelle didn't have much time for reflection that day. Emma and Pete launched into filming, based on the format they'd already worked out in London. Chantelle took them round the estate for background scenes, and lots of Remondins introduced themselves, posing obligingly for family scenes. Heloise could be interviewed later.

'After the big party, I think,' Chantelle decided. 'I don't think I'll get her full attention before then.'

No-one called Marie appeared, and after several false sightings — there was a strong familial likeness in the male branch of the Remondins — to her relief, Phillipe didn't appear. Nor did Joelle. She concluded that they were together somewhere, and dreaded the inevitable meeting with them the next day.

In her sumptuous bedroom, even grander than the one allocated to her before, she undid the shutters to let in the scented night air. The chateau had quietened, and everybody seemed to be in bed early, ready for the next day's events. As Chantelle worked on the documentary script, finalising minor points, she heard a scrunch of gravel in the distance, and got up to see who was arriving at such a late hour. She wondered if it could be Phillipe and Joelle.

Leaning out over the sill, she saw, parked below in the courtyard, the mysterious, black limousine, a uniformed chauffeur holding open the passenger door. A tall, dark-suited man got out. There was a glint of silver hair, and then he was gone, hurrying into the house.

Thoughtfully, Chantelle returned to work, determined to finish before she went to bed. Half an hour later, she realised that a tape with vital information was downstairs with Pete's camera equipment. She remembered putting it on top of his case. She glanced at her watch — midnight. Not too late.

Cautiously, she stepped into the long corridor. Night lights lit her way to the head of the stairs but the hall and downstairs was ablaze with light. The equipment was in the library. The door was ajar, but as Chantelle crossed the hall towards it, she heard voices, which increased in volume as she drew near.

She caught snatches of conversation, recognising Heloise and Madame

Plombier, then over-riding the two women's voices, a rich baritone.

'She's right, Heloise. It's time to let go. We weren't meant to suffer this long . . . you're making yourself ill . . . too much . . . haven't asked if . . . Phillipe . . . punished . . . Marie was unstable . . . Joelle . . . her life.'

The fragments didn't make much sense, and Heloise was talking rapidly, with rising inflection across the other two, who were trying to calm her. Chantelle stood uncertainly, outside the door. She needed the tape, but she didn't want to eavesdrop. Manufacturing a loud cough, she knocked at the door.

The voices ceased at once, and Madame Plombier appeared in the doorway. 'Mademoiselle Wilde!' Her voice was cold, shocked.

'I'm — er — sorry. I'm working. I left a tape in here.'

'Where is it? I'll get it. Stay there,' she commanded.

'It's by the camera equipment,'

Chantelle said, wishing she was safely back in her room.

'Come in, Chantelle.' Heloise's voice over-rode her secretary's.

With a murmured, 'I'm sorry,' Chantelle slipped into the room, and took the tape from Madame Plombier.

There were three people in the room — the frowning Madame Plombier, Heloise, sitting very upright in a high-backed chair, and the man, unmistakably the one she'd seen getting out of the limousine. With a shock, she recognised him and a name she'd heard when she first arrived clicked into place — Monsieur Beaugendre! He was, even at seventy plus, very attractive; his face, strong and handsome, his hair thick silver-white.

Intelligent, shrewd eyes looked at Chantelle quizzically and kindly. 'You are working very late, mademoiselle. You're from Newsworld, I presume?'

'Yes. I'm so sorry to have disturbed you,' she stuttered.

André Beaugendre! The charismatic

and influential politician she'd read so much about in her college course on French Modern History — where on earth did he fit into the Remondin set-up?

'No problem.' He patted Heloise's shoulder. 'It's time we were all asleep. You have a big day tomorrow, my dear. You should rest.'

Heloise moved impatiently. 'I wish you would all stop treating me like a sick child. I shall be perfectly all right. Good-night, Chantelle.' She nodded dismissively, and Chantelle slipped away quickly, but not before she'd seen André Beaugendre's fine eyes narrow with concern.

*　*　*

The chateau was alive and stirring just before dawn. A milky sky heralded a fine, hot day, and final preparations were in full flow as the sun began to rise above the huge marquee, now ready for the main ball that evening. Already, long tables were being set on the lawns beneath the trees for the family lunch. Servants and family all seemed to have plenty to do. Emma and Pete were busy, and would be fully occupied during the day.

Chantelle wandered away from the chateau, across the parklands towards the fields. It was quiet and peaceful among the vines, now laden with grapes, just beginning to turn from hard green to pinky purple. She wondered how far away the river was. It hadn't seemed far when she was on the back of Phillipe's motor bike, but she wasn't sure of the direction.

She walked on, imagining the cool waters of the bathing spot, and wondered again about André Beaugendre. He was famous — or notorious, depending on your political viewpoint — as a key figure in the students' riots in Paris in the Sixties. Radical, fiery, a born leader, he had disappeared from public eye for a while, but emerged as a formidable force in French political life, to take high office in the Seventies and Eighties. Now he was an elder statesman of considerable reputation. Chantelle wondered about the whispers of scandal around Heloise's past. Did André Beaugendre hold the key?

The sound of rippling water cut across her thoughts. The river was just ahead of her. It was pure bliss to sit on the bank, dangling her feet in the cool water. It was wonderfully tranquil with only the sharp sweetness of bird song harmonising with the trickling water — until a familiar voice jerked her into reality.

'Chantelle!'

She turned. It was, inevitably, Phillipe, and as she looked up at him, staring directly into his grey eyes, she knew, without doubt, that she had been deceiving herself during the past weeks. The carefully-erected barriers around her heart crumbled and vanished.

'Phillipe,' she whispered, shading her eyes against the sun to see him more clearly. She saw him put out his hands, taking hers, and raising her to her feet. His face was dark, intense, his eyes burning into hers.

'I prayed you wouldn't come,' he said hoarsely.

Mesmerised, she stared up at him. 'I didn't want to. Tim insisted . . . '

Then it was too late. Phillipe drew her to him, and kissed her passionately. She struggled, but all her strength had left her. With a gasp, she swayed against him, and they remained locked, close together.

She was only conscious of her pounding blood, Phillipe's strong body, and warm lips. Powerless, lost in bittersweet sensation, she wanted the kiss to continue for ever. It was Phillipe who finally raised his head, but his hold didn't slacken.

'Chantelle!' His voice was ragged. 'You can't marry Michel Deschamps.'

For a second, Chantelle wondered who Michel Deschamps was, her reasoning completely obliterated by the pounding passion coursing through her.

'I . . . ' she began.

Then there was a voice, loud and urgent, nearby.

'Phillipe, where are you? Phillipe . . . ' A young man emerged through the trees, carrying spraying equipment. He was dressed in the dungarees of an estate worker, and stopped abruptly as he saw them. He hesitated. 'Phillipe — I — just wanted to ask. The vines in the lower field . . . '

Chantelle almost fell as Phillipe released her.

'Raoul! What are you doing here?'

The dark-haired man looked at him curiously. 'We agreed, don't you remember? The spraying — before the party. They're about to begin lunch, by the way. You'll be late.'

'Damn!' The dark eyes drew together as Phillipe looked at Chantelle. 'I must go straightaway.'

'Joelle's already there,' Raoul said.

Then Chantelle remembered. Resentment and shame overwhelmed her and with as much dignity as she could muster, she drew herself up, saying loudly and defiantly, 'Yes, of course. You must go back to your fiancée — ' and to make sure she got her message across, she added defiantly, 'And I **am** going to marry Michel Deschamps!'

9

Chantelle stood well back in the shade of a huge chestnut tree, watching the Remondin clan at mid-day lunch. It was an idyllic setting for the family occasion. The family ages ranged from eight to eighty, with a couple of babes in arms passed affectionately from one lap to another. Pete was filming the scene discreetly.

Although there was lots of chatter, gesticulations and happy laughter, Chantelle sensed the tensions. Heloise, at the head of the table, looked beautiful and there was no sign of the sick woman, apart from a nervous clenching and unclenching of one hand resting on the table. Phillipe, on her right, looked grim, while Joelle, on her left, had downcast eyes. André Beau-gendre, somewhere around the middle, cast anxious glances towards Heloise.

The atmosphere at the adjoining table was more relaxed. Jacques Remondin, the prodigal son visiting from Australia, was apparently unaware of any of the conflicts and kept his party going with a swing. The noise level rose steadily.

At last, Chantelle could bear it no longer. As the festivities continued, she crept away quietly to the cool haven of her room, where she lay on her bed, closed her eyes and tried to calm her racing heart. She squeezed her eyelids tightly together, trying to blot out the sight of Phillipe by the river, of her own wild response to his embrace — the sort of embrace which belonged to Joelle.

Mercifully, she drifted off into a troubled doze. She woke with a start, as Emma burst into her room.

'Chantelle! How can you sleep? There's so much going on outside. All sorts of people arriving. Fabulous dresses. There's champagne at six o'clock, for family and friends — then all the estate workers and villagers. The mayor'll be at the six o'clock affair. Chantelle, do wake up, you're missing it all.'

If only I could miss it, Chantelle thought, struggling upright, blinking at the glamorous vision before her. Emma was dressed in full evening regalia, a long, white, silk dress setting off her black hair perfectly.

'Oh, come on, Chantelle. What's the matter? What are you going to wear? Can't let Newsworld down.'

'I aim to blend into the background. If you'll go and let me shower, I'll meet you downstairs.' Emma bounced away happily, leaving Chantelle alone.

Her floating, blue chiffon dress heightened the sapphire beauty of Chantelle's eyes. She pulled her thick hair into a knot, but curly tendrils escaped, framing her tanned face.

'You look beautiful,' Emma whispered to her when they met downstairs.

'We're here to work,' Chantelle reminded her.

'OK, I'm trailing Pete. See you later.'

Chantelle had left it as late as she dared to join the cocktail throng and already people were moving away through the fairy-lit garden, towards the marquee. Music from a sedate chamber orchestra, soon to be replaced by the wilder beat of the disco, floated from the terrace.

Jacques Remondin came up to her, his grey eyes approving. 'You look very charming, Chantelle. A perfect English rose.'

Her brain jarred at the echo. Had the nephew inherited the Gallic charm act from his uncle? But Jacques' grey eyes were perfectly sincere.

He handed her a glass of champagne. 'You must toast the evening. Every year I come home, I cannot believe it when we have all this. I think Maman likes to create a film set — maybe to remind her . . . ' He was silent for a second then went on, 'Excuse me, I must find my wife. You'll dance with me later, I hope?'

She made her way slowly towards the marquee, which had been set up as a night club with tables arranged round a dance floor. She found a small table, tucked away almost behind the band, for herself, Emma and Pete. But she wasn't allowed to remain a quiet observer. Jacques claimed a dance, as did countless other Remondins and villagers. It soon became overpoweringly hot.

Heloise and the older members of the family sat at a special table on a raised platform. A roving spotlight frequently picked out Heloise, magnificent in dark green silk, with flashing emeralds to match. André Beaugendre was at her table.

Suddenly, Phillipe was standing over her, darkly handsome in a white evening jacket and black trousers.

'Dance with me,' he said softly.

She turned away. 'No, thank you.' Her voice was cold.

'Chantelle!' He took her arm. 'Please, I have to talk to you.'

'No! Never again.' She tried to shake free, but his grip held. 'Let me go.'

'No.' He pulled her to her feet but at that moment the music died away.

'Look,' Chantelle hissed. 'Your grandmother's calling you. She has Joelle with her. Go — where you belong.'

Spotlights illuminated Heloise's table. She was standing, staring directly at her grandson, commanding him with her eyes. A spotlight picked him out. With a last look at Chantelle, he obeyed his grandmother's silent summons.

A hush fell in the crowded marquee as Heloise began to speak. It was her annual command performance, and she held her audience of family and friends spellbound. Her speech was fairly mundane with many thank-yous, references to family happenings and village events but her charisma was undiminished. She could have read the local wine list and everyone would have listened, spellbound by the resonant theatrical voice. After ten minutes, she began to falter. She was tiring. Phillipe moved towards her, but she gestured him away.

'Now, my most pleasurable announcement. I've left it until the end — to savour, like all good and blessed things.' She turned to Phillipe, took his hand, and drew Joelle up from the chair near her. 'Tonight, the culmination of my dearest wish. The formal announcement of my grandson's engagement — to my ward, Joelle Vivier. Their destiny was in the stars at their births. They will fulfil that destiny on their wedding day in one month, here at the Chateau Remondin, when we will repeat this grand occasion. But then, the leading players will be — Phillipe and Joelle!'

There was a moment's silence, then a burst of prolonged clapping from the audience. The music played, and the buzz of conversation dissolved as the crowd began to dance again.

Chantelle's eyes remained rivetted on the platform. Phillipe was arguing with Heloise. Joelle, eyes wide and scared, stood back. André Beaugendre moved swiftly to stand by Heloise. Phillipe's eyes were blazing as he spoke to his grandmother. He said something to the band leader who motioned his group to suspend the noisy beat.

The crowd murmured and turned back to the platform as Phillipe took the microphone. Heloise plucked at his sleeve, but he ignored her. Then Joelle screamed as Madame Remondin, hands clasped to her side, slid slowly to the floor in a crumpled heap.

Chantelle, on tip-toe, couldn't see what happened next. Bodies bent over Heloise, were urged back, space was cleared. Someone, presumably a local doctor, leaped on to the platform, and sent someone running out of the marquee.

André Beaugendre took charge. He grabbed the microphone, and spoke authoritatively. 'Madame Remondin is ill. An ambulance has been sent for. Please stay as quiet as possible.'

'Pete,' Chantelle said shortly, 'put

that camera down.'

Shame-faced, he did so. 'Sorry. Automatic reaction.'

'Let's go. This is a family affair. We've no place here.'

The guests were already beginning to leave, and Chantelle looked back to the platform as she went to join them. At that same moment, Phillipe raised his head and met her eyes. The look he gave her was dark, unfathomable and bitter. Already, in the distance, the wail of the ambulance could be heard.

★　★　★

Two hours later, the grounds were dark, the house quiet, and the party mood had vanished. Most of the guests had left but a few hung on for news. Phillipe had gone in the ambulance, along with Madame Plombier, followed by Jacques and André Beaugendre by car.

Later, Phillipe telephoned a message that Heloise had had a heart attack. Her condition was poor, but there was nothing to do but wait. Everyone, he suggested, should go to bed and pray. Most people followed his advice, but a few, unable to settle, made coffee before eventually drifting off to their rooms.

Of the young people, only Joelle remained. Wide awake and tearful, she clung unaccountably to Chantelle, following her around, asking her to stay with her, at least until Phillipe came back. She was acting like someone who was carrying a huge burden of guilt.

Even as the thought crossed Chantelle's mind, the younger girl blurted out, 'Chantelle — if Madame Remondin dies, it'll be my fault.'

Chantelle blinked, alarmed, though she managed to hide it. One person in a panic was enough to cope with at a time.

'Of course, it won't,' she said, calmly. 'Heloise has not been well for a while. How could it be your fault? And she won't die, I'm sure of it.'

The girl looked haunted, and grasped Chantelle's hand tightly. 'I can't keep quiet any longer. I've got to talk to someone.'

Why me, Chantelle thought, as Joelle began to sob uncontrollably.

'I've got to tell you.' Huge, wracking sobs tore from her, but just then, to Chantelle's relief, car headlights outside flashed around the room.

Joelle sprang up.

'They're back.' She clutched Chantelle's hand even tighter, her eyes fixed on the door.

The three men came in slowly, Phillipe first, startled to see Joelle so close to Chantelle. Joelle went to him, and he put his arms round her.

'She is holding her own,' he said quickly.

Chantelle looked away. 'I'm glad,' she said, and got up to go.

'Don't leave. I want you to listen to something Monsieur Beaugendre has to say.' Madame Plombier, sober faced, had followed the men into the room. 'Marie, could you get us some brandy please? Joelle, you look as though you need it. Chantelle, you, too?'

She shook her head. 'I should go. This is a family concern, not mine.'

Phillipe's laugh was a shade bitter. 'Well, almost, though it appears that's what we've thought all these years, Marie.'

Suddenly the name registered in Chantelle's brain.

Marie Plombier! Surely she wasn't the Marie . . . ? What had she overheard? 'Marie was unstable . . . Marie wouldn't have allowed it . . . if we don't obey . . . '

Jacques Remondin interrupted her thoughts as he came to sit by her on the sofa. 'None of the family knew — all those years ago . . . '

'Please, Uncle,' Phillipe interrupted, 'let André tell his story. I want no-one else in the family to hear of this. Chantelle, I have to trust you. This is definitely not for Newsworld. It's a private matter. But you — you are involved.'

She looked at him rebelliously. What right had he to ask for her trust? He'd betrayed hers over and over.

He came over and took her hand. 'Chantelle, I asked you to trust me once before; you didn't, and our stupid pride has led us into this mess. Please, trust me this time.'

The plea in his eyes was irresistible. She had no option but to stay and listen to André Beaugendre's story.

10

It was three o'clock in the morning, but no-one suggested that he keep his story until the next day. André Beaugendre looked at the pale, strained faces of his small audience.

Joelle sat close to Phillipe. She was still crying, but more quietly, and as André began to speak, her sobs gradually subsided, her eyes fixed intently on the older man's face.

Hesitantly at first, he began to speak. He nodded towards Chantelle. 'My credentials for being here are two-fold, Miss Wilde. I commissioned your documentary on Madame Remondin's work and life, for reasons I will explain presently. But the main reason I am here, confessing to her family for the first time, is that Heloise and I have been in love for over thirty years. I told Jacques and Phillipe this in the car coming back from the hospital. What they do not know are the circumstances. Madame Plombier — Marie — is the only person who has known from the beginning.' He glanced towards her, standing by the door. 'Won't you come and sit down, Marie? You must be worn out.'

Grudgingly, she perched on the edge of a chair, well away from the main group, as if to keep herself apart from the proceedings.

André went on. 'I met Heloise two years after she was widowed. She was in her late thirties, had had three children and achieved dazzling stardom. I was married to Marie.'

Chantelle started. Was this the same Marie whom Heloise had mentioned?

André hesitated, a flicker of pain clouding his expression. 'I must tell you, though in no way as an excuse for what happened, that Marie, my wife, was as unstable as she was beautiful and my highly-strung, young bride quickly turned into a neurotic, severely depressed woman.'

He added heavily, 'She was also pregnant when I went to a reception at the embassy in Paris, and saw Heloise Remondin for the first time. You can have no idea of the impact of that meeting. She was unbelievable! A year out of mourning for her late husband, she had a quality, a charisma, which I can't describe.' He broke off, the emotion of that long-ago time remembered clearly.

Phillipe said softly, 'She still has it.'

André recovered, speaking rapidly now, as though to exorcise a burden he'd carried for thirty years. 'If I thought, for one moment, that Heloise would die, I should never speak of these things, but she will live, and we must help her to be free from the shadow of the tragic events that started on that night in Paris when we fell in love — instantly and irrevocably. We fought it, for a time. Marie was increasingly unwell, and given to fits of despair. I tried to help her, but she seemed to turn against us all — even her own family. Inevitably, Heloise and I became lovers.' He lifted his head, and looked squarely at her family. 'You must know the powerful pull of deep, passionate love. I am not ashamed of it.'

André continued. 'Our love was fated always to be clouded by guilt and secrecy, but when we were together, our joy and happiness was overwhelming. We could not plan a future, but neither could we imagine a future without each other. We lived from day to day, snatching secret moments from our busy lives.'

He coughed, and Chantelle saw the pain darken his eyes.

'In the end, it was Marie who decided our future. A well-meaning friend told her of our affair. She was insanely jealous, threatened to expose us and ruin our careers unless we gave each other up. You young people may find it hard to understand, but in those days, scandal could wreck careers, especially a woman's, and we were both dedicated — I to politics and Heloise to her acting. She had a young family to consider and I, a duty to my wife. So we decided to part. I promised Marie I would never see Heloise again. But we had to have a last time together. That was a mistake, although it was the happiest week of my life.'

He continued firmly, determinedly. 'But we intended to keep our word to Marie, who seemed calmer for a while, more reasonable. She gave birth to our daughter, but then refused to feed her, or even see her. The doctors diagnosed post-natal depression, and said she would come out of it in time, but they didn't know Marie, or how desperately sick she was. Apparently that same well-meaning friend had learned of my final farewell with Heloise and our last precious days together. Marie believed we had betrayed her and planned a terrible and bizarre revenge — and, I believe, lost her reason completely.'

Phillipe got up and touched his shoulder. 'You're exhausted. Do you

181

'want to rest for a while?'

'No, I must finish. And I can't rest until we hear from the hospital. I have to go back to her.' The old man's voice was hoarse with emotion.

Phillipe poured a small amount of brandy into André's glass and sat down again by Joelle. Every eye was on André as he went on.

'Marie went to her lawyer and drew up a document willing her daughter to Heloise. There were all sorts of crazy stipulations. The child was to be brought up in a family home. Heloise was to give up her career. For as long as we both lived, we were to be jointly responsible for the child and its descendants, but Heloise had to adopt the baby legally. I was to remain in the background.'

'But that's madness,' Jacques broke in. 'No court would uphold that. And what about Marie's own family?'

André held up his hand. 'Wait. Let me finish. You, perhaps, have little experience of the power exerted beyond the grave. That was Marie's intention. In her twisted, paranoid, unhappy mind, I think she intended to ruin Heloise's career, and to bind us together in mutual recrimination — and eventual hatred. In the latter, she failed. When the baby was four weeks old, Marie dressed herself in her wedding gown, tied its long veil around her neck, attached the other end to a rail, and threw herself over the stair-well. She'd chosen her moment well. The nanny had taken the baby to the clinic, and the house was empty. I found Marie, still hanging there, when I came home.'

There was a gasp, then shocked silence. Chantelle's eyes blurred with tears for the sad, dead girl. Joelle leaned against Phillipe, shocked horror in her face.

No-one spoke, except André, hurrying on, driving himself to continue his saga to the bitter end. 'The suicide was hushed up by her family. Post-natal depression — a convenient peg. Then her lawyer told me of her will. Marie's account of our affair, to be released to the Press if we didn't do exactly as she demanded was lurid and sensational — and mostly invented. A letter to Heloise was delivered personally by her lawyer before I could intercept it. That letter has blighted and distorted our lives from that moment to this. Marie condemned Heloise, and threatened retribution from the grave if her wishes were not carried out to the letter.'

'A terrible vengeance,' Jacques said quietly, 'but surely, a woman of Maman's intelligence . . . '

'Intelligence? Rational thought flew out of the window, I fear,' André replied quietly. 'Marie made sure her end was dramatic enough to scar her rival for life. Heloise's agony and guilt were enormous. She was forced to do as Marie wished and end her career, and weld the family unit together to contain Gisaine.'

'Gisaine was your daughter? We always believed she was an orphan.' Jacques leaned forward.

Joelle's voice was hardly audible. 'She was my mother, wasn't she? I know it. You're my grandfather.'

André's look of agony made Chantelle's heart turn over. 'Yes.'

Joelle jumped up. 'All these years — why did you let me believe I was an orphan, someone Heloise took pity on? I always knew it wasn't true! Why didn't you tell me?'

André looked at her with infinite sadness. 'My dear, don't you think I didn't want to?'

'Then . . . '

'Please, let me finish. Then you can judge — condemn — what you will.'

Phillipe took Joelle's arm, and drew her back to sit beside him.

'Heloise made her choice, though in her mind, there was no option. It was forced upon her, and she hated that. She finished her last film, 'Princess In Exile,' then bought Chateau Remondin, here in the heart of the country, where I could visit, as a family friend, from time to time. We remained in love, as deeply as ever, but never became lovers again. Marie's demonic trust saw to that. Heloise devoted herself to her family and gradually accepted her new rôle. Life gradually settled down.'

Phillipe said, 'So Grandmère didn't actually choose family before career?'

André shrugged. 'Without Marie's curse there would have been no reason to give up. Many stars combine career and motherhood. But it was a great sacrifice for her, and after fifteen years of seclusion, I asked her to think of returning to films or the stage. She'd had enough offers over the years. And I asked her to marry me — the strength of Marie's vengeance was losing its hold on her mind as life went quietly by. Heloise, at last, agreed, but she asked me to wait a year, until Gisaine was sixteen. I was so happy at the prospect of our marriage, I would have agreed to anything.'

He sighed quietly. 'We planned to announce our engagement on Gisaine's sixteenth birthday, and to tell Gisaine who her parents were. Well.' He nodded to Jacques. 'You will know the rest. In that year, Gisaine became a difficult and rebellious teenager, and ran away. You probably didn't know we eventually found her, pregnant, in a Paris squat, abandoned by the child's father. Gisaine, my daughter, whom I'd never acknowledged, died giving birth to Joelle, my granddaughter.'

He looked appealingly at Joelle, who stared back at him wide-eyed. His gaze fell away, and now every word was an effort, dragged from a soul weary of the torment and unease of the last decades.

'Heloise refused absolutely to marry me. She referred to Gisaine's death as Marie's curse, and from then on, was obsessed by the need to do as she thought Marie would have wished. I was to have no claim on Gisaine's child — she would adopt the baby herself.'

André sat back in his chair, drained. 'The rest is well known Remondin history. Heloise's carefully reconstructed life continued to fall apart. You, Jacques, albeit with your mother's blessing, emigrated to Australia — the beginning of another rocky road for Heloise. In the mid-Seventies, Phillipe's mother and father, and Fleur, Heloise's oldest daughter, were drowned at sea. Nothing would, or will now, convince Heloise that the family tragedies aren't a direct result of Marie's evil-wishing. She is terrified for her family — and for you especially, Joelle. That's why you have to marry Phillipe. In her eyes, right or wrong, it's the only way to keep you safe.'

'Grandmère — Maman,' Joelle whispered, tears streaming from her eyes.

Phillipe put his arms around her, and rocked her like a child, his eyes seeking, and holding, Chantelle's, his expression unfathomable.

'You must remember,' André said wearily, 'Heloise is a born actress, with the temperament to match. She's volatile, superstitious, and lately she's become obsessed with the notion that Marie's spirit has returned to haunt her. She thinks Joelle will only be safe with you, Phillipe, because it's within the family — the demonic trust!' Now he looked exhausted, but said to Chantelle, 'I tried to persuade Heloise to bring it all into the open — exorcise the spirit. I suppose I have thought that if Newsworld made a film about her, it would stimulate some sort of action — uncover, examine and then bury the old scandal — blow away Marie's ghost. I was wrong.'

'But it did,' Chantelle said. 'The Press in London got hold of something . . . '

'I put a stop to that,' Phillipe said grimly. 'I threatened a libel suit. Why didn't you tell us all this before, André? We could have helped her so much more.'

'It's easy to be wise when it's too late. Now she can't rest until she thinks Joelle has been taken care of. If you don't marry it will break her heart — if she recovers.'

And it will break mine if you do, Chantelle cried silently.

Pale fingers of dawn light were creeping around the closed shutters. No-one said a word until Marie Plombier stepped forward, her face wet with tears. 'I believe, between you all, you've already killed her. She . . . '

'Marie!' André's sharp reprimand was cut off by the shrilling of the telephone.

Jacques ran out of the room. They all listened tensely to his terse replies. Then he returned. 'The doctor thinks we should go to the hospital — at once.'

★ ★ ★

Chantelle sat on her bed, numbed by André Beaugendre's story. So Phillipe was obligated to marry Joelle. Did he love her — or she him? The anguish that had been in Joelle's eyes had been grief for her dead mother's tale, and for her grandparents — but there was something else there, too — something Chantelle couldn't quite put her finger on. Fear? Defiance? Resentment?

190

Slowly she undressed, put on a thin, cotton night-shirt, and lay under the covers. They'd pack up and go as soon as she'd had a sleep. Chateau Remondin was no place for a camera crew — whatever the outcome.

There was a knock, the door opened quietly and Phillipe came in.

'Chantelle? You're not asleep?'

'Phillipe! Shouldn't you be at the hospital?'

'We're going. I had to see you.' His grey eyes showed the strain of the past hours. His hair was rumpled, and his mouth was taut. He came over to the bed, sat down and took her hands. 'Chantelle, I must know. Is it really true that you're engaged to Michel Deschamps? Are you going to marry him?'

Her heart was hammering so loudly, he must surely hear it. A slow flush spread from her bare shoulders to her cheeks. She lowered her eyelids. 'Yes.'

There was a long pause, then Phillipe released her hands. Her head drooped lower, then was jerked up again as his fingers dug into her shoulders, and he shook her roughly.

'Chantelle, for goodness' sake — forget your stupid pride. It's important that you tell me the truth. When you kissed me this morning I knew you couldn't love Michel, and I don't believe that you are a woman who plays games with me.' His eyes blazed into hers, and she couldn't look away from him. 'You have to say it to me — that you love Michel Deschamps.'

Chantelle knew she was beaten. She took a deep breath, and looked into his eyes. 'No, I don't love Michel. I'm not engaged to him. It was all a mistake — a lie because you were — are — to marry Joelle,' she finished miserably.

Then she folded in his arms. He kissed her. 'Thank God. I have to go now but you must promise me that this time you really will trust me. You see the circumstances — it's delicate. Joelle is . . . I can't explain, but you must trust me.' He tilted her face to his, and his eyes, now the soft grey of a dove's wing, pleaded with hers. 'Our future depends on it. Promise.'

'I promise,' she said.

He kissed her again, then with a despairing groan, broke away. 'If you knew how hard it is for me to leave you!' He kissed her once more, then was gone.

A few minutes later, she heard the screech of tyres outside and she imagined the red sports car speeding off towards the hospital.

★ ★ ★

She slept and awoke to bright daylight. Her watch read one o'clock. She shot out of bed, all the events of the previous evening tumbling back into her brain. She touched her lips. Had she imagined that last visit of Phillipe's? She couldn't have — the memory of his kisses was imprinted on her mouth. She was glad she'd told him about Michel.

She went downstairs. No-one was about. Either they'd left, gone to the hospital, or were into the mid-day siesta. Outside, workmen were already dismantling the marquee.

She found Emma and Pete sitting under the big chestnut tree, sipping mineral water. Pete groaned as she came to sit by them. 'I've got a terrible hangover. What happened last night, after Madame had been carried off?'

'Oh, family things,' Chantelle said vaguely. 'What's the news? How is she?'

'I don't know. We haven't been up long. I kept hearing telephones ring — lots of doors banging — then, when I got up, Emma was here. The chateau's deserted now!'

'We should go back to England, I think,' Emma said anxiously.

'We haven't got the Heloise Remondin interview,' Pete wailed.

'Not much chance of that now.' Chantelle stood up. 'I have to see Phillipe once more. After that, we'll get moving. I'm going in to pack.'

'Me, too — when I can move.' Pete flopped back on to the grass. 'Coffee would be wonderful.'

'I'll get you some.' Emma laughed. 'I hope the old lady's all right. She's quite a performer, isn't she?'

Chantelle had to agree.

Madame Plombier was standing by the library door as Chantelle went indoors. 'Miss Wilde, I've been looking for you everywhere.'

'Madame Remondin — how is she — have you heard?'

'Of course. I've been with her. The crisis is over.'

'Thank goodness. I'm so glad.'

Marie Plombier smiled at her. 'Yes, she'll be all right now. You see, Joelle and Phillipe were married by special licence at the hospital. She told me she saw the marriage certificate. Now, if you'll excuse me, I have to pack some things to take to her.' As she swept away, she called out over her shoulder, 'I expect you'll be leaving now.' Her voice was triumphant.

Trust me, he'd said. Chantelle couldn't believe it. How could he and

Joelle be married so quickly? Why had he come back to see her, to ask about Michel? What possible interest could it be to him, if he was set on marrying Joelle? With a choked cry, she ran upstairs to her room, and began throwing things into a suitcase, wildly, not seeing what she was doing. The faster she was out of Chateau Remondin the better. Pete would have to forgo his coffee. She rammed the case shut, and ran downstairs, colliding with Emma and Pete.

'Quickly, we're going,' she said.

'What's the rush? I thought we'd see if there was any lunch left. I feel better after coffee.' Pete looked bewildered.

'Now!' Chantelle was stern. 'I'll buy you lunch on the road.'

'OK, OK. I'll get my stuff.'

'I'll see you outside in ten minutes. If you're not there, I'm going, with the car.'

She went out into the sunshine, which now seemed mockingly over-bright. She shaded her eyes, and put her case down. The red car was in the drive, and Phillipe was coming towards her, his face grim.

He looked pointedly at her case. 'Running out again?'

'There's no reason for me to stay.'

'Oh, there is. You aren't going anywhere yet.' He swept her up in his arms, bundled her into the back of his car, sprinted round to the driver's seat, slammed the door, and accelerated towards the vineyards.

'Let me out, Phillipe.' Chantelle banged her fists on his back.

'Sorry. It's the only way with you, apparently. Stop flailing about or we'll have an accident.'

The car juddered along the same track the motor bike had taken so many months ago. Chantelle stopped struggling.

'That's better.' He turned and smiled at her and she could tell that at least Marie Plombier had spoken the truth about Heloise's recovery. The bleak, despairing anxiety had gone from Phillipe's eyes.

He stopped the car and lifted her out as if she was a feather, and didn't put her down until they'd reached the flat rock by the picnic pool. Then he carefully set her on her feet and took her in his arms.

'Didn't I say trust me? Why were you running away? Don't you realise how I feel about you, Chantelle?'

'How can I trust you?' she flashed angrily. 'You tell me one thing — someone else tells me . . . '

'That someone wouldn't be Marie Plombier by any chance? I guessed that. She's as mad as that other Marie. But you have to forgive her — she's so devoted to my grandmother, she's blinkered to anything but what Heloise wants, so if it doesn't happen that way, she invents it.'

'She said you and Joelle were married at the hospital. Today . . . '

Phillipe stopped her, his mouth claiming hers in tender passion. He kissed her deeply. When he raised his head, his eloquent eyes told her the truth. 'Chantelle, I am not married to Joelle. I never could be. For one thing, she's already married, for another, I'm going to marry you. I love you, Chantelle. That should have been obvious from the very first day we met.'

'How on earth — Joelle married?' But her heart sang its own joyful song as he kissed her again.

He drew her down to sit beside him on the sun-kissed rock, the dappled water murmuring its accompaniment to the words which were such music in her ears.

'I love you,' he repeated, 'and you love me, don't you? Say it, Chantelle. Forget everything else.'

She raised her dark blue eyes to his, and said simply, 'I love you, Phillipe.'

He kissed her again, until she was breathless, her body weak with a delicious fervour of its own. 'Phillipe, you must explain it. Heloise . . . '

'Will get better, I promise. She was and still is very ill. After what André told us, we decided we had to act out our own charade. She had a heart attack, brought on by stress and anxiety. As soon as Joelle and I promised to marry, she seemed better, but she was sedated — still confused. Time meant nothing to her. So we pretended we'd gone through the ceremony — and for her sake, Chantelle, we even showed her a marriage certificate.'

'What?'

'Ssh, it was Joelle's. Grandmère wasn't well enough to notice that the bridegroom's name was Raoul Latour.'

'Raoul!' Chantelle gasped with shock.

'Joelle and Raoul have been in love for a long time, but Heloise wouldn't hear of their marrying. I think that's when her obsession started — about Joelle and me. We pretended to go along with it, to divert attention from Joelle and Raoul. Now I see it was foolish. We've all been wrong — we've been too frightened of upsetting Grandmère. Now we know the truth, we must help her to forget the past, and face the future.

'André will take his proper place in

her life. He loves her so much. Joelle has lived too long in Heloise's shadow. She was so scared that she and Raoul eloped and kept their marriage secret. It was Raoul who finally made her tell me a week ago. I think Grandmère suspected something, but denied it to herself, and started to live in a fantasy world — aided by Marie Plombier, of course. We were going to tell Grandmère after the celebrations, when all the family had left. Now it's in the open.'

'But why didn't you tell me that you and Joelle weren't engaged?' Chantelle cried, thinking of her days of anguish, weeks they'd wasted.

'Hush, cherie.' He silenced her with a tender kiss. 'I was going to. Remember I came racing back from Lyon especially — but you told me you were to be married. And when I saw you in Nice with Michel . . . ' His arms tightened around her. 'But that, like Heloise's secret, is in the past. We, you and I, are the future, part of the Remondin future which Grandmère will come to accept.'

Chantelle heard the birds singing, and the quiet splashing of the nearby waterfall, but all she saw was the man she loved with all her being — and who was looking at her with such a world of love in his own eyes, that she reached up and kissed him, pulling his dark head down to hers. For a while, they sat entwined in each others arms.

Then Phillipe reluctantly put her from him. 'We have to go back, my dearest. There's still so much to do. I must telephone the hospital. I wish the two of us could be alone together. You'll stay on?'

'No. We'll go back to London today,' Chantelle said gently. 'Heloise is important. You have to be with her until she's well enough to . . . '

'Come to our wedding,' he exclaimed. 'It must be soon, Chantelle. At the chateau.'

'Only if Heloise . . . '

He pulled her to her feet, and embraced her tightly.

'I promise you that Grandmère will be at our wedding, here at the chateau.

All the family will gather again — Uncle Jacques from Australia — André, Betsy, Pierre, Francine, even Michel, and the whole of Newsworld.'

'Stop, stop, Phillipe!'

He interrupted with slow emphasis. 'But the best part will be when just you and I leave the crowds behind — just the two of us — together for always. Trust me. It will happen.'

His lips claimed hers, and Chantelle knew it would be as Phillipe said. She would return to Chateau Remondin in the very near future, and then would be happy together for ever in the sunlight of her beloved Provence.

The End

We do hope that you have enjoyed reading this large print book.

Did you know that all of our titles are available for purchase?

We publish a wide range of high quality large print books including:
Romances, Mysteries, Classics
General Fiction
Non Fiction and Westerns

Special interest titles available in large print are:
The Little Oxford Dictionary
Music Book, Song Book
Hymn Book, Service Book

Also available from us courtesy of Oxford University Press:
Young Readers' Dictionary
(large print edition)
Young Readers' Thesaurus
(large print edition)

For further information or a free brochure, please contact us at:
Ulverscroft Large Print Books Ltd.,
The Green, Bradgate Road, Anstey,
Leicester, LE7 7FU, England.
Tel: (00 44) **0116 236 4325**
Fax: (00 44) **0116 234 0205**

Other titles in the
Linford Romance Library:

A FAMILY AFFAIR

Mel Vincent

When Harriet Maxwell, a divorced headteacher, spends the summer with her family in Spain, she falls in love with Carlos Mendoza: a widower with four children. But Harriet faces a dilemma: Zoe, her teenaged daughter, also falls for Carlos; the forthcoming marriage announcement cannot be made. Her predicament gets complicated when a misunderstanding prompts Carlos to leave. As Harriet copes with various family problems, and bonds with his children, she fears she will never see Carlos again.

LOVE IS A NEW WORLD

Helen Sharp

When Elizabeth Carleton met Jake Bartlett, Rolfe Sumner's farm-hand, her life changed forever. Despite her thinking him handsome, he was still a hired man. But in sleepy Washington, Vermont, Elizabeth found herself loving him, agreeing to marry him and becoming the owner of Sumner farm. And when she discovered Jake's dark secret, she fought to win him back from the edge of habitual bleakness — and won. For Liz, the summer she met Jake was the summer that changed her forever.

PLANTAGENET PRINCESS

Hilda Brookman Stanier

Elizabeth of York is a controversial figure. Did she or did she not love her Uncle Richard? What was the relationship between herself and Margaret Beaufort, her mother-in-law? How much affection did Henry VII have for the niece of the man whose throne he had usurped by right of conquest? This book attempts to answer these questions and gain an insight into the life of Elizabeth of York.

THE FAMILY AT MILL HOUSE

Bryony Dene

Anna, unhappy after breaking off her engagement to the charming Bruce Grayson, leaves the city to teach in a Wiltshire village. However, she faces new problems and tensions when she becomes involved with the family at Mill House: Guy Deering, an embittered widower, his bored sister and his difficult child, Peter. How did Bruce and Guy know one another? What was the mystery surrounding Helen Deering's death? When Anna finds the answers, she also finds love and happiness.